Ladies of the Night

also by the author
Loving This Man
Being Black

Ladies of the Night

stories
Althea Prince

INSOMNIAC PRESS

Library and Archives Canada Cataloguing in Publication

Prince, Althea, 1945-
Ladies of the night / Althea Prince.

Originally published under title: Ladies of the night and other stories.
Toronto : Sister Vision, 1993.
ISBN 1-894663-98-5

1. Women, Black--Fiction. 2. Women, Black--Fiction. I. Title.

PS8581.R549L3 2005   C813'.54   C2005-903422-X

The publisher gratefully acknowledges the support of the Canada Council, the Ontario Arts Council and the Department of Canadian Heritage through the Book Publishing Industry Development Program.

Insomniac Press
192 Spadina Avenue, Suite 403
Toronto, Ontario, Canada, M5T 2C2
www.insomniacpress.com

This new edition is dedicated to the memory of my friend, Arah (Junie) Hector with whom I shared secrets in girlhood and adulthood.

Thank you to the editorial and production staff at Insomniac Press for taking care of this elegant new edition. I especially thank the publisher, Mike O'Connor, and the managing editor, Dan Varrette. It was pleasurable bringing this book to publication.

A few words to start...

While the characters in all of these stories reside only in my fictive imagination, I have strong appreciation for women who talk their story, no matter how it makes some people wince. One may flinch from the pain in one story, and move to embrace another that reconciles love.

Contents

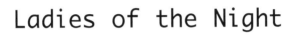

Ladies of the Night

Their petals open softly in the dark
The Ladies of the Night
Waking up when needed
To sweeten the horrors of the night
That no one's taken back

They sweeten the dank, dark scents
When everyone sleeps ...
... all but the night soil men

Are these jobs open to women?

I went back there.

There was a time I left
... thinking no one knew me when ...

Now I peer at the faces
Hoping for no recognition
And finding instead ... a fine, fine madness ...
... thinly disguised as gladness
If only I had seen it way back then
When my spirit ached for arms to hold me
Reaching out through the thick, thick darkness
Of the night

Then I moved in the shadow
My heart in a hollow, loving so
Seeking to follow in footsteps ...
Some too deep, some too shallow
How I loved so ...
And ached so ... and wanted so

Sun setting in a west sky, touching sea ...
... caressing land

Do men and women love so ... here?
Then why do they hate so? hit so? leave so?
Is there a malaise of commitment?
Me hear so, dem say so, nuh mus so make so?

Moon watching on a dark-dark night
Behind a cloud, a silver shroud
He wooed her, protected her, then released her
Defenceless to the wolves
Nuh just so does make so?
Nuh you must know ah so make so?

If only I had seen it way back then
When their petals opened softly in the dark
The Ladies of the Night
Waking up when needed
To sweeten the horrors of the night
That no one's taken back.

Ladies of the Night

Miss Peggy had been whoring ever since she could remember, and she felt no shame about it. "It takes one to know one," she said whenever anybody called her a whore.

She was not certain, but she had a feeling that she did her first whoring when she was maybe less than twelve years old. Her mother, Miss Olive, always pretended she could not remember how old her daughter had been when she lost her cherry. Eventually Miss Peggy got tired of asking Miss Olive about it. She got tired because her mother's only answer would be, "Me doan member dose tings." Then she would suck her teeth, going "choopse" in disgust at being asked such a question.

Miss Peggy knew her mother was lying, knew she just did not want to admit anything. Maybe it was the way Miss Olive darted her eyes whenever her daughter asked her that question that made the lies so obvious.

Deciding that it was best to leave the topic alone, Miss Peggy could see her mother's embarrassment behind the shifting eyes and angry voice. Embarrassment was not a feeling Miss Olive showed often to her daughter, but Miss Peggy knew her mother so well that there was nothing she could hide from her.

Miss Olive could have admitted the truth because it would have made no difference to Miss Peggy, who enjoyed whoring and felt a certain pride at how early she began to have power over men. She remembered her mother calling out to her as she played with some stones in the yard, "Peggy, come child, come go wid dis man. He have money to give you." Peggy had thrown away her stones and had gone inside their little house with the man.

She had not realised what was expected of her until the weight of the man was on her thin body and she found herself pressed into the sagging bed. She had screamed as he entered her, and he had put a big hand over her mouth. When the man had put his pants back on and left the house, Peggy had got up. Feeling ragged inside herself, she had crept outside to her mother. The man was nowhere in sight, and she had run to her mother, tears streaming down her face, a five-dollar bill clutched in her hand.

"Is no big ting, chile. You have to do it sometime, so take it easy. I going wash you off."

Then she had looked at the money that her daughter still clutched in her hand. "How much money he give you?" she had asked. Peggy had extended her hand and opened her fist to reveal the five-dollar bill. Miss Olive had smiled. "Five dollars! And is you first time. Well, well!"

Peggy had felt a little better at having made her mother smile at her. She did not really understand how she had managed to secure so much money, but she was happy she had pleased her mother. Pleasing her mother was her major task in life at the time. Mostly she failed at it and waited for the shower of blows that always came with Miss Olive's disapproval. Little Peggy had watched as her mother added the five-dollar bill to a twenty-dollar bill in her purse but did not know that her mother had also been rewarded by the man.

Now Peggy was grown up and was called "Miss" just like her mother. She felt stronger than Miss Olive, for she knew that she was better at getting money from men than her mother had ever been. She only dealt with men of High Society, men who were from the upper classes and who were mostly light-skinned. She also serviced calypsonians from Trinidad when they came to Antigua to put on shows at Carnival time.

Her customers and the goods Miss Peggy bought with her body made her the envy of the neighbourhood. Her neighbours were not prepared, however, to pay what she paid, and they would insult Miss Peggy when they saw her and call out at her as she walked down the street, "Whoring Miss Peggy!" That was when she would retort, "It takes one to know one!"

Now that Miss Olive was old and could no longer ply her trade, Miss Peggy looked after her. She set her up with a tray, and Miss Olive sat outside their little house on a chair with the tray on a box and sold snacks to people as they passed down the street. The tray held sweets, cigarettes and chocolates. Sometimes when Miss Peggy was in the mood she would even parch peanuts in hot sand in a doving pot and package them in little brown paper bags for the tray. Or she would make "suck-a-bubbies"—sweetened, flavoured milk squares—in the freezer of her refrigerator.

Miss Olive felt proud of Miss Peggy, but would curse her at the slightest provocation, and there was never a day that went by when she did not find reason to be provoked. The surrounding area would ring with her harsh voice, and sometimes people would stop and listen on their way to the market or to town, but they would soon become bored and move on because Miss Olive always cursed her daughter about the same topics: Miss Peggy's love of men and her love of money. Everyone in the neighbourhood found it strange that Miss Peggy, the biggest curser in the area, never ever answered her mother.

One day everything changed.

It started off like any other day. Everything went as usual until the early part of the afternoon. Miss Olive was sitting outside at the front of the house, minding her tray and brushing flies with a whisk brush. As the flies circled the tray she would switch the whisk from one hand to the other, the tail of the whisk making a massaging sound as she kept the flies on the move.

Miss Peggy was inside the house with a regular, twice-a-week customer—the only customer that Miss Peggy ever fed. He was eating goat-water, and the smell of the stewed goat meat filled the street. He was the same man who had paid her five dollars to have sex when she was a little girl.

Miss Peggy went outside and asked Miss Olive for a cigarette from the open package on the tray. Miss Olive's answer was sharp and immediate: "You not tired feed dat man and give him me cigarette? Why he don't go home to his wife and ask she for cigarette and food?" Then she sucked her teeth with a resounding "choopse," still brushing at the flies throughout.

Miss Peggy stood in front of the tray, watching her mother for a full minute. Then she asked again for a cigarette and Miss Olive went "choopse" again, ignoring her. She switched her whisk brush from one hand to the other, indicating she was busy and was not going to give Miss Peggy the cigarette. The nonchalant swoosh, swoosh, of the whisk meant Miss Olive had dismissed her.

Miss Peggy charged into Miss Olive and her tray. She bit her and punched her and slapped her. The man ran out of the house and tried to hold Miss Peggy, but there was no stopping her. She picked up a stone and used it to beat Miss Olive's back. A neighbour left his tailor shop and ran, his tape measure swinging around his neck, to call the police. Nobody could stop Miss Peggy and everybody knew it. Neighbours came and tried and gave up, standing by helplessly while Miss Peggy beat her mother to the ground.

Some people were laughing and passing comments as the beating continued: "Lord me God, is what happen to dis woman?" "But dis is a crazy woman!"

One woman said to Miss Peggy, "Miss Peggy, you is a advantage-taker. You is a young woman to you mother. How you beat she so?" She said it over and over as if the repetition would make Miss Peggy stop. It was no use. Miss Peggy continued to beat away at Miss Olive as if she were tenderizing conchs. Then she sat on Miss Olive's legs and ripped off her clothes. As the old woman lay naked on the ground Miss Peggy scratched at her and slapped her. Miss Olive moaned loudly while she tried to cover her nakedness and protect her face from her daughter's nails.

The neighbours found it doubly strange that Miss Olive, known for her fighting skills, did so little to defend herself from Miss Peggy's blows. She could not have done much anyway, but she did not even try; she just moaned or grunted at each blow and tried to dodge them. And Miss Peggy, known for her talk, did not say anything at all while she was beating her mother. She grunted like a wild pig and just kept on hitting her, sometimes holding onto Miss Olive and digging her teeth into her arm or her shoulder. She drew blood, spat it out and dug her teeth into another part of her mother's body. It was the worst beating the neighbourhood had ever seen. It was also the first time they had seen a woman bite someone. It was unusual for a daughter to beat her mother, let alone bite her.

As the beating continued, Miss Peggy began to tire. She then switched to using only her head on her mother. She butted her in the stomach, and Miss Olive made a sound like a live lobster in a pot of boiling water. Then Miss Olive fainted.

Still Miss Peggy beat her mother, only now she cried as she beat her. When the police came it took three burly policemen and four of the men standing in the street to pull Miss Peggy off her now unconscious mother. Miss Olive was taken to the hospital in shock, and Miss Peggy was locked up for the night in the police station. The next day, when the police took Miss Olive home from the hospital, they asked her if she wanted to lay a charge against her daughter. Miss Olive refused, and Miss Peggy was charged only with causing a disturbance.

After the fight Miss Peggy and Miss Olive stopped speaking to each other, but they continued to live together. Miss Olive started to cook Miss Peggy's favourite foods on Sundays. And during the week, Miss Peggy did all the cooking so Miss Olive could mind her tray. Before the fight Miss Peggy would insist that Miss Olive could cook and mind the tray at the same time. She claimed that she did not have time to cook as she was busy with her clients. She brought in most of the money and could not be expected to interrupt her work to cook.

Now Miss Peggy cooked willingly every morning before she began to work, and if Miss Olive tried to make a meal, Miss Peggy would firmly take the pot from her without a word and do the cooking herself. Miss Olive would look pleased but would say nothing as she went about setting out her tray on the ground outside.

After the fight Miss Olive began to do all the ironing. Before the beating she used to insist that Miss Peggy had to look after her own clothes. Miss Olive even washed all the clothes on some days, although the soap powder gave her a rash on her hands. Without a murmur of complaint she would rub her hands with Vaseline after she did the washing. One day Miss Peggy brought home a bottle of sweet-smelling hand cream and wordlessly handed it to her mother. Miss Olive's face softened as she took the gift, but she said nothing. It was, said the neighbours, some kind of peace.

Two or three months after the fight Miss Peggy and Miss Olive began to go to church and take Communion every Sunday. They did this with no discussion between them. People in the neighbourhood knew that although they were going to church together, they were still not speaking to each other. The first Sunday they left the house at the same time, both dressed to kill. Neighbours came to their windows to watch Miss Peggy and Miss Olive walk up the street. As the two women passed the little Sunday market on the corner, all heads turned and people stopped haggling over prices to watch.

"Is what church coming to?" Miss Tiny said loudly as Miss Peggy and Miss Olive walked past her tray of mangoes, "Lord have mercy!"

Everyone laughed at Miss Tiny's comment, and Miss Olive

and Miss Peggy edged closer to each other as they heard the laughter, but still they did not speak to each other. Their arrival at the church caused as much stir as the walk through the neighbourhood had done. The minister was very disturbed by the presence of the two best-known whores in Antigua at his Communion rail and had several long talks with God in private during the service. But neither the minister nor God seemed to be able to do anything about Miss Olive and Miss Peggy being in church that Sunday morning or any other Sunday morning. Worse yet, neither could do anything about them walking up to the Communion rail, heads held high.

Miss Olive and Miss Peggy continued to present themselves at the eight o'clock service every Sunday. Piously they would walk up the aisle for the body and blood of the Lord, opening their mouths wide as the minister concluded, "which was given for you." After they took their sip of wine the minister would surreptitiously wipe the chalice most carefully and then spin it to a fresh spot before presenting it to his more respectable communicants.

Things went on like this for many years. Then Miss Olive died. One morning Miss Peggy noticed her mother had not got up at her usual time, and she went over to her bed and shook her. Miss Peggy screamed and started crying, and when a neighbour came running to see what was wrong, she sobbed, "Me mother dead. Lord me belly, me belly. Me mother dead an ah never tell her ah sorry."

After her mother's death Miss Peggy would struggle to find her speech, then sigh and drop her shoulders and say nothing. She did not even speak to the men she serviced regularly. When with Miss Peggy the men felt as if they were taking advantage of her. Eventually they left her and moved on to the new houses where the new whores from the Dominican Republic lived. At least they spoke to their clients, even though it was in Spanish. They laughed, too, and sang along with the music on the juke box.

Only one man continued to come to see Miss Peggy, and he gave her money every week though he no longer touched her. He was the man she cooked for at least twice a week, the five-dollar man at the centre of the fight between Miss Peggy and Miss Olive. Over the years he came to see Miss Peggy every day. When he got old and could hardly walk he still visited her, leaning heavily on a cane as he shuffled down the street to Miss Peggy's house. He no longer went inside when he visited but would sit outside on the little bench where Miss Olive used to sit and mind her tray.

Miss Peggy now relied on selling from the tray to earn her livelihood. While she tended her tray her friend would sit on the bench and watch people passing by. Miss Peggy would sit on the steps silently, happy in his company. The man seemed very comfortable sitting there with Miss Peggy. He did not seem to need to speak.

Miss Peggy would look happier when the man came to visit her, and she would fuss over him and cook for him and go to the shop and hold up two fingers to indicate to the shop-keeper that she wanted two cigarettes. After the man had eaten she would offer him the cigarettes, and while he smoked she sipped her cup of chocolate tea. It was an easy, comfortable friendship between the old man and Miss Peggy, still a young woman in her thirties.

Several years later the man died. Miss Peggy found out

about it when his death was announced on the radio. All his children and grandchildren were listed in the death announcement, and Miss Peggy wondered how it was that a man who had so much family used to be so lonely that he would come and spend every evening with her. She cried sadly when she heard the radio announcement and could not even bring herself to eat her lunch. She went back into her bed and kept her windows closed. Late in the afternoon, there was a knock on Miss Peggy's door and she jumped up from her sleep, almost expecting it to be her friend. She had been dreaming about him, and it was around the time of afternoon that he used to visit her. Then she remembered he had died. Her heart felt heavy with grief as she came fully awake.

She went to her door to answer the persistent knocking and saw a man wearing a suit standing on her step. He asked to come in and speak with her, telling her that he was her friend's lawyer. Miss Peggy let him into her little house, wondering what he could want with her. The lawyer explained that she had been named in the man's will. She was to receive money to look after her for the rest of her life. That part of the will, he said, was very clear. He gave Miss Peggy a strange look and began to read from the paper in his hand: "And for my beloved daughter whom I sired with Olive Barnabus, who is called: Peggy Sheila Barnabus, I bequeath the following. ..."

Miss Peggy went back in her mind to the first day she lay in a bed with the man whom she had come to call her friend. She remembered how he left her ragged inside. She remembered, too, how her mother had rejoiced at the five dollars he had given Miss Peggy. She had known deep down inside that her mother had been jealous of her friendship with him, and

Miss Peggy had secretly enjoyed her jealousy. "My beloved daughter whom I sired with Olive Barnabus." Miss Peggy's mind went over the words again and again while the lawyer continued to read the terms and conditions of the will. She did not understand all that he said and could not find her voice to ask any questions she might have had.

At the funeral Miss Peggy stood on the sidelines listening to the hymns. In her hand she clutched a bouquet of ladies of the night she had begged from Mrs. Sebastian on her way up the street to the cathedral. Some people in the funeral party knew her and knew of her friendship with the dead man. Others assumed her to be one of the family's servants. The few dark-skinned people at the funeral could be accounted for, so Miss Peggy stood out. She noticed some questioning looks and became uncomfortable. It was not a big funeral, so there was no buffering crowd Miss Peggy could melt into. When the first sod was thrown on the coffin she left quietly, hoping that no one noticed her departure.

As she left the grave she passed a handkerchief she had wet with bay rum over her forehead, then she held it to her nose and her mouth. She felt faint, but she walked with determination to another part of the cemetery, where she searched the headstones until she found her mother's grave buried among weeds and grass. She bent down and pulled up the weeds crowding the lilies of the valley she had planted there after the last rainy season. She pulled one blossom from the bouquet of flowers in her hand and gently pressed it into the sod at the place she knew her mother's head rested.

"He dead, mother. He dead," Miss Peggy said, bending to pull a weed. She sat by her mother's grave until the mourners had left the cemetery, then walked to the other grave, where she sat down. Laying her bouquet of flowers at the head of the grave, she kissed her fingers and pressed them into the soft sod.

"Goodbye," she said softly, then got up and brushed the graveyard dirt off her dress and her shoes and set off for home. She unlocked the padlock and threw open the wooden door, letting the soft evening sun into the little house. Then, drawing back the curtains and opening the windows, she threw open the shutters to let in more sun. Her voice was strong and lilting as she sang, *Why should I feel discouraged? / Why should the shadows fall? / Why should my heart be lonely?* She paused only to change into her home clothes before continuing, *For Jesus is my potion / My constant friend is He / I sing because I'm happy / I sing because I'm free / His eyes are on the sparrow / and I know He watches me.*

She finished changing her clothes and put her tray outside next to the bench that first her mother and then her father used to sit on as she sang, *Whenever I am tempted / Whenever clouds I see ...* Then Miss Peggy laughed a sweet joyous laugh. She sat on the little bench and took up her mother's whisk brush as a group of children walked past. One threw a little pebble at the house and shouted "Whoring Miss Peggy!" before the group raced down the street. Miss Peggy set down her whisk brush carefully. She got up from the bench and walked into the street. Putting her arms on her hips, she bellowed, "Whore like you mothers! It takes one to know one!"

Henrietta

Flamboyant red, bougainvillea purple—splashes of colour against the fence of galvanized wrecks and pieces of rotting board. The old woman who lived in the house behind the fence pulled herself out of her house by holding onto the doorway.

The children who wrote to her three times a year from Canada were a constant lament in Henrietta's mind. She was not sure if it was worth it to read their letters but collected the little slips of paper the postman brought on her birthdays and at Christmastime that were marked "Registered mail for Miss Henrietta Nathaniel." Each time the postman reminded her that she would get money if she took the slips of paper to the post office.

Henrietta did not understand why her children could not send the money directly to her. No, they so contrary, she thought, that they send slips of paper. Then she would have to go to the post office and sign and get somebody in there to say that she was the same person as the name on the envelope.

She shook her head and sighed, remembering the last time she went to the post office and waited while they decided if she was the right person to receive the money. By then Henrietta's legs were hurting her so badly that she was sure she would faint in the post office and make a big to-do right in the middle of town. She had done that two times already, and was not doing it again. She shook her head and grunted, "Hmm! Let them use de money to bury me"; she was sure that one more trip to the post office would kill her.

Henrietta went outside to light her coal pot and make her tea. "Life so hard sometimes," she muttered as she put the shavings on top of the coals and lit them with a match. She had just enough coals to boil the water. She picked some noo-noo balsam and put it in her cup, then put her water on to boil and went to the shop to get her bread.

She took her time going to the shop; her knees were hurting her, so she walked carefully. So much hole in de sidewalk and de street was no better. She bought her bread, a half-ounce of margarine and half-ounce of cheese, then walked back home, taking care not to stumble.

The postman had put a letter under her door; it was from Pammie, her daughter. She wrote she would be home on the 24th of July. That's tomorrow! Henrietta realised excitedly as she looked at the little calendar Pammie had sent her from Canada last Christmas.

Pammie had come home for Carnival last year too. She had stayed with her friends in a big wall-house, in some place called Paradise Hill, out by All Saints way. Henrietta didn't know for sure where it was, but she remembered how Pammie would come and see her every morning in a car with her friends. They would wait outside with the car engine running, and when Pammie had stayed inside talking with her for a short while, they would blow the car horn and shout, "Pam-ell-la!" Pam-ell-la would answer back, "Comm-in-ing!"

"Next ting me know," Henrietta muttered to herself. "Pammie gone with them 'til next day, after she push some guilt-money in me hand. Gone to Paradise." Life hard for old people here, Henrietta thought, as she poured boiling water on the bush in her cup. Pammie said there should be some plan for old people so they wouldn't have it so hard when dey couldn't work any more.

Henrietta had not planned on struggling so hard after she had raised her four boys and her girl. "So pretty, too, Pammie," she sighed as she thought about her daughter.

Henrietta had worked all of her life for Mistress Withers in Silver Grove. She used to walk to Silver Grove from town every morning, leaving home at half-past five, hurrying to reach there in time to cook the breakfast. Then she would leave after six in the evening, when she had finished preparing the dinner. That was before she was old and weak. She used to be able to walk fast then too. Now she could hardly walk.

One day Mistress Withers told her, "Henrietta, you're getting old, you should stay home and rest. I'm hiring a younger woman next week. I will always give you something to keep you, in between your children helping you out." Just like that Henrietta had found herself at home. That was five years ago, and she had never seen nor heard from Mistress Withers since that day.

Truly she did have a hard time getting herself to Silver Grove more than a few days a week. She used to arrive there after ten o'clock in the morning. By then Mistress Withers would have already made the breakfast and eaten it. Henrietta remembered how she used to make bacon and eggs, toast, juice, cream of wheat and coffee.

Henrietta sat on her chair to eat her breakfast. She cut her bread open, buttered it with margarine and put cheese on it. The bush tea was still drawing, and she sighed with pleasure at the smell of the noo-noo balsam.

Pammie arrived home for Carnival the next day and went to visit her mother as usual. Her friends waited in the car with the engine running. Soon they tooted the car horn and shouted as usual, "Pam-ell-la!"

Pammie never heard the car horn, nor did she hear the car leave. She knelt weeping over the stiff figure of her mother whose fingers were curled around her cold cup of bush-tea with a drowned roach lying in it. In her other hand she held a piece of bread and cheese, which was covered with an army of ants.

Croops, Croops, Croops

Croops, croops, croops. The sound of clothes washing had fascinated her when she was a little girl. She had tried since she was five years old to wash with that croops, croops, croops sound. She would wash her dolls' clothes and try to make her hands move in the same way that Hopie, the old woman who washed for her mother, moved her hands. She thought if she could wash the way Hopie did, she, too, could make the clothes go croops, croops, croops.

She used to sit on a big stone in the yard next to Hopie and put her dolls' clothes into the basin of soapy water Hopie had given her. She rubbed them like Hopie rubbed the clothes in the big bath pan, listening for that pretty sound—croops, croops, croops— but instead the clothes would make a slippery splish sound. "It was like cooking," the big people told her as she grew older, "like cooking fungie or rice and peas." You either knew through some mysterious woman's wisdom how to turn fungie and how to cook grainy rice, or you did not.

The words stayed with her as she grew up: "If you can't wash, if you can't turn fungie, and you can't make grainy rice, no man will want to marry you, cause you not a real woman."

"She can't cook!" was the ultimate indictment. If a man left his wife and got a keep-woman whose food warmed his belly, a woman who did his washing, he had done no wrong. How could he be blamed if his wife was not a real woman?

Even the wife's own women friends and women relatives would say behind her back: "What she expect? She can't wash, she fungie lumpy, lumpy, and she cook rice like pap. What she expect?"

"You have to turn you fungie in such a way dat it don't have in it any lumps," her mother often told her while she demonstrated the art. And you had to see the okra peeping out at regular intervals, like the holes in a man's white merino. The balls of fungie should be smooth and yellow. That was real fungie, cooked by a real woman. "If dey black," her mother would say, as she turned the corn-meal, "is because you let de okra-water boil too long."

She could still hear her mother's voice, "You rice should have peas in it—either red beans or pigeon peas or black-eye peas. De pot must have just enough grease, a little piece of pig-mouth or salt beef and de rice should be grainy."

To make clothes go croops, croops, croops, to cook fungie with okra peeping out of it like a man's holey merino; to serve grainy rice and peas—that is what real women did. She had failed at each and had worried about getting a man to marry her, for truly she was not a real woman. She could not cook and she could not wash the right way. She did not enjoy being around children either. So what man would marry her?

She grew up and stopped worrying about what man would marry her. She no longer cared to acquire the virtues of a real woman. On the contrary, she took pleasure that she was not a real woman and had no desire to take up the drudgery of croops, croops, croops, smooth fungie, grainy rice and the obligations of motherhood.

She told her lovers, "I can't wash to suit you, I can't cook fungie to suit you and I cook rice like pap, but I want to love you and be loved by you." Her lovers found her refreshing, then went home to wives who washed their pants and shirts, their merinos and their undershorts, making the dried-up evidence of their time with her melt into the soapy water. Croops, croops, croops. Hands washing, washing, washing. Lunch of fungie and saltfish. Pieces of okra peeping out of the yellow ball of fungie. Grainy rice with peas. A piece of pig-tail or salt beef nesting on top of the rice next to the fish or the back-and-neck. Hands cooking, cooking, cooking. Husbands eating, eating, eating with a hunger born out of the time spent with her.

It had only been a week, but it seemed it had been so long since Cintie felt the ground beneath her feet. Today felt like all the other bad days.

She got up and turned on the radio. All she could find were Spanish stations. Too early, she thought, moving away from the radio. I might as well go back to bed. She was afraid to do that because having made it to her feet, she did not want to risk lying on the mattress. It was like that some days. At dawn a heavy ache would come over her and she would feel that floating feeling. It would be the middle of the day by the time she got up again. She would note the time with surprise and stumble back to bed, staying there until late afternoon. Sometimes she would cry softly as she lay in bed, missing her husband so much her belly hurt.

She was puzzled by these feelings. She had been happy to be rid of him. He had packed his clothes in their one battered suitcase on a Friday evening and walked out the door. They had quarrelled violently, one in a series that each took days to blow over.

"I can't take any more," he had said as he packed his clothes. "A man must have some peace. You is a nag and I don't care if I never see you again. You middle name is Misery. Life is more than this miserableness you does give."

He banged the door behind him as he left and it kept banging itself in and out. She had watched it for a few minutes, half expecting to see him re-enter the house. She did not believe he was serious because he always turned around when he reached the street.

As Cintie sat looking at the door, she thought it looked exhausted, like her. The door had needed fixing for months, but Samuel had never found the time to fix it. Now, like Cintie, it was still. She had thought she would find it a relief not to expect attention, for her and for the door. She was rid of him, rid of quarrels, rid of cooking for him, washing for him, picking up after him. All she did was wash, wash, wash and cook, cook, cook. Then he would come home and eat, eat, eat.

What hurt her was that when she was washing Samuel's clothes she would come across evidence that he had been with another woman. She would soak his undershorts in two sets of water, trying without touching them too much to get out the remains of his love-making with another woman. One day she solved the problem by leaving his week's worth of dirty undershorts out of the wash. Eventually, of course, he ran out of clean undershorts and came asking her, "Cintie, how come I don't have any clean undershorts? Where all'a them?"

"Look them right dey in de dirty clothes bundle," she said.

"They full of you an you woman and me not washing them."

Samuel was caught and he knew it. He had never expected her to notice, and he himself had not known there was caked sperm in his undershorts. He used to take them off when he came home and put on the old pants that he slept in. He realised now that by morning the undershorts would have caked and dried. All those years Cintie must have seen it, but she had never said anything, just lay in wait for him. He said as much to her.

She said evenly, "Everybody make dey own excuse, eh? If I did quarrel and stop washing for you long time you would say that me wicked and worthless. You ever stop to think it's just too much? You ever think 'bout that?"

So it was that from that day Samuel started to wash his own undershorts. He washed them late in the evening and picked them up off the line early the next morning so none of the neighbours would see he had been washing. Then he hung them up, still damp with dew, inside the house over the bedroom door.

Cintie would be annoyed about that, too, because they made a damp smell in the little house, and not only that, they were left there for days because Samuel never remembered to put them away in the suitcase with his clothes. She would see them first thing in the morning and last thing at night—constant reminders of his time with that woman. When Samuel ran out of undershorts again Cintie would watch as he took the clean ones down and hung up the next set.

How she could miss a man who was so barefaced about his woman? How she could miss his always eating, eating, eating? He would come home from his woman, hungry like a dog that had been running a race. Earlier she would have cooked their dinner, wondering if it would be just her and her daughter eating together. Some evenings Samuel came straight home from work. Those nights he would be nice to her, talking and laughing, asking, "Where Tracey? She gone to choir practice or she playing netball?"

Tracey was thirteen years old. Most of the time she felt sorry for her parents because they seemed so unhappy together. She felt sorry for her mother in particular because she saw her cry when her father was out all evening, coming home just in time to eat and go to sleep. She loved her father best, though. He took the time to joke with her in the morning when they ate breakfast and on the nights he came home instead of going to his woman. Her mother was always sad or angry, and Tracey only saw her smile or laugh when she was happy with her father.

Tracey knew her father's woman, knew where she lived, too, because she saw her father's truck parked outside the woman's house all the time. Tracey thought the woman dressed nicely and kept herself looking good. She was slim, like Tracey's mother, and she was black-skinned with a round face that looked almost like a little girl's. Tracey found her rather good-looking, although she felt that her mother was far more beautiful.

Her mother was jet-black, with smooth, smooth skin. Her hair was thick and she kept it in four big plaits bumped up on her head. She had cat eyes that were clear and shiny when she was happy, especially when Tracey's father spent the whole night at home. Tracey did not sleep those nights. From her bed on a piece of sponge on the floor in the front room she would listen through the low partition to them making love in the bedroom.

When Tracey was little she could not figure out what they were doing together that made them whisper and made their bed squeak and groan, so she used to go back to sleep. As she grew older she knew her parents were doing *IT*, the *IT* she whispered and giggled about with her friends. Mornings after the nights of whisperings, groanings and squeakings were always special. Her mother and father would be nice to each other and to her. Sometimes there would be several days of niceness, with her father coming home every day right after work. No undershorts hung inside the house and her mother would sing as she washed, the clothes going croops, croops, croops in her hands.

Then without warning her father would come home after dark. Undershorts would hang over the bedroom door for days and her mother's eyes would grow dull. Tracey would seek her friends for solace, wishing for her parents to be nice with each other again.

Cintie had thought that when Samuel left she would go about her life and feel peace. Instead she felt lonely and found herself wanting her husband's long muscular body next to hers at night. She began to think about how he had never slept out since they were married. She remembered how he had looked after her when she was pregnant with Tracey and she was too sick to cook. The smell of the food on the fire would make her vomit, so Samuel would cook special fish broths for her, with a grunt or a grouper head. He would put in ground provisions and *cruffy cucumber* just the way she liked it.

She remembered him coaxing her to eat and sitting with

her at the table while she belched up gas from not eating any-thing since the breakfast he had also fed her. He didn't have a woman then. Afterwards he would make her a cup of green tea. Later he would help her as she tried to undress herself, unbuttoning her blouse at the back, heating up some water for her to have a sponge bath before going to sleep, lifting her breasts so she could wipe them, kissing them gently because they were heavy, then helping her to sit in the basin so she could wash off. Always helping her, helping her, helping her.

Her tears soaked her face as she cried softly in the early morn-ing. So he have a woman, so what dat mean? It mean that he don't love me anymore? No, Samuel still love me, I know that.

"Every man in this island have a woman," he used to say. "That don't mean anything, Cintie. You still my queen. You so nice, I wouldn't leave you. Me love you like me love meself. When you going understand that? Stop worrying over stupidness."

She would half-believe him, then she would see his woman in town and she would feel shabby because the woman had changed into her nice clothes to go in the street, dressed like one of the bank girls, though she did domestic work like Cintie. Whenever the woman saw Cintie she would walk fast to get out of her sight because she was afraid of her. But Cintie had no quarrel with the woman, though the sight of her made her skin hot. Her quarrel was with Samuel, who had promised to forsake all others and cleave unto her. That is what marriage meant. People said that over and over and deep down that is what she had thought it would be like to be married.

Each time she saw the woman Cintie would make Samuel's life miserable for days. "I see you little choopse of a woman in town today." Samuel's shoulders would slump and then straighten as he braced himself. "She dress up as if she going party. Is you buying all them clothes? Samuel, you not shame? A grown man with a big daughter, keeping a woman, buying she clothes, paying she bills. You not shame?"

By now the question had become fact. "Samuel, how you going keep two house? You planning to leave me? Is that you planning? Samuel, answer me, you dawg."

If Tracey was at home, Samuel would talk to her, hoping to kill Cintie's anger by ignoring it.

"Samuel, you dawg, is you I talking to. So tell me, how you going feel living with you woman, leaving you legal wife? Eh, Samuel? Tell me."

Conjecture, too, became fact, and finally Samuel's fury would unleash itself. "Cintie, you is a real crazy woman, you know. Me tell you me going live with any woman? Because is your house you want tell me leave? Me can leave, you know. Don't pull no style on me, girl."

Tracey would leave them to quarrel it out. That night there would be no creaking bed, no whispers, no laughter; the next morning there would be silence or more quarrelling, depending on her mother's mood and her father's response. Tracey grew used to it. Sometimes she would try to ease the tension between her parents by making them laugh. Her mother and father would look at each other uneasily; sometimes her father would hug her mother, then she would tell him to leave her alone, that he was too bad. Samuel would cajole her, holding her around her waist, pulling her close to him while winking at a smiling Tracey.

Tracey loved those times, but when her attempts at reconciliation did not work she would set off to the street pipe for water or to school with a heavy heart. Only her friends' chatter on the way to school could lift her spirits. Coming home, she would wonder if her parents would be speaking to each other when her father got home.

The night her father moved out Tracey was not home. She had gone to stay in the country with her aunt for the month of August. Tracey came home on a Sunday. As she walked into the yard she noticed that there was no cooking going on, even though it was noon. Normally they had Sunday lunch at two o'clock and by now the peas for the rice should have been cooking on the coal pot. Tracey knew that sometimes her mother would boil the white clothes in the big pan until it was time to cook lunch. This Sunday there was no water boiling in the big pan and the coal pot was not even outside.

As Tracey came up to the house she wondered if her mother had gone to church. What she saw as she entered the house frightened her. Her mother lay on the floor on Tracey's sponge bed, fully dressed, her legs curled up with her knees touching her chest. Her eyes were closed, but she was crying softly, her tears running down her face.

"Mother, what happen? Where Daddy?"

Cintie stopped crying at the sound of her daughter's voice, looking up at Tracey with red, swollen eyes. She had lain on her left side all morning, and now her right arm was puffy with mosquito bites. She did not answer at first, just sat up on the low bed, scratched her head, then rubbed her arm. She stood up shakily and Tracey rushed to hold her up.

"What happen, mother. Why you crying?" Cintie could not speak. She felt dizzy and weak as she had eaten nothing all day. Finally she said in a dull, tight voice, "You father gorn. He move out three weeks ago and living wid his woman."

Tracey felt dizzy. "Daddy gorn! How you mean he gorn? What make him leave? He gorn for good?" Tracey let go of her mother, who was now crying softly again.

Tracey loved her mother. They had a closeness like two women friends, and though her mother never talked about her father, Tracey knew that she loved him. She could tell from the way she prepared his food, the way she washed and ironed his clothes, the way her eyes lit up when he came home, the way she listened for his step in the yard, the way she hurt whenever she saw his woman in town, the way she giggled when they whispered together in the darkened bedroom at night.

She said to her mother, "I going make some tea for you." She kissed her. "Don't cry any more, mother. Daddy coming back; he not going live with any woman. All-you just vex with each other for now."

Tracey made the tea and left her mother sipping it while she put on the peas to boil. As she went about soaking a package of frozen chicken wings for lunch, she tumbled their predicament over and over in her mind. Soon, she thought of a plan: she would go to the woman's house and find her father and make him come home.

Daddy you can't leave me and mother, she thought as she worked; you can't leave us just so. She was frightened and nervous, for what she was about to do was not going to be easy. She was just thirteen years old, a girl dipping into big people's story, but she wanted her father back, and her mother was getting crazy.

She remembered a prayer from church. "Lord have mercy upon us," Tracey prayed. "Christ have mercy upon us." It was part of the Communion service, and she always used to think it comical when the choir sang it on Sunday mornings in the Anglican Cathedral. She said it over and over in her head now, finding that it brought her a feeling that she was getting help from God.

The peas were bubbling in the pot and the chicken wings still soaking when Tracey said to her mother, "I coming back now," and set off for the woman's house. Her mother sipped her tea and sat looking at the floor. She was so sad-looking, the sight of her pulled at Tracey's heart; it was as if all of the fight had gone out of her.

Tracey let herself out the gate and was sure that if her mother listened, she would hear her heart beating thump, thump. As she walked down the sidewalk, she saw each house clearly, and she noticed the brightness of the sun. She saw each hibiscus bush, each soursop tree, and all of the croten bushes along the way. Everything looked sharper than it had before.

She said good afternoon to Mr. Joseph as he sat on the step outside of his house, noticing for the first time that his glasses had tortoise-shell frames. Her eyes took in his blue cotton shirt and his freshly pressed khaki pants, with a seam that could cut you like a knife. Miss Amy was drawing water at the street pipe, and Tracey noticed for the first time that she was so bowlegged that it made her seem short. One part of her mind kept taking pictures snap, snap, snap at things that were not important while another part trembled at what she was setting out to do.

At the woman's house the front door was wide open. There were pretty pink curtains blowing at the window. Her father's truck was parked outside, and her mind took a picture of that, too, as she knocked on the front door. She rapped loudly because there was music playing inside, loud reggae music, and the singer's voice rang in her ears: *We're stealing love on the side / you don't belong to me / I don't belong to you.* Tracey laughed crazily at the irony of the words of the song.

There was laughter from inside of the house, too—a woman's laughter, like a tinkly set of bells. You can't steal my daddy, Tracey thought as she rapped again, louder this time. The woman came to the open door from the bedroom.

"Where my daddy?" Tracey asked, looking at the bedroom door.

"He not here," the woman said.

"He here because his truck here," Tracey retorted, decidedly and deliberately hostile.

"He leave his truck here, but he not here." The woman looked at Tracey carefully, then added, "He leave say he coming back soon."

Tracey knew that her daddy would have come out of the bedroom if he had heard her voice. She turned abruptly away and ran down the steps, but once she had taken only a few steps away from the house she changed her mind and turned back. She went to her father's truck and leaned on it, waiting for him. The trembling had moved from inside her belly to her legs, shaking her knees so much that she leaned heavily on the truck for support.

Soon her father came walking down the street. At first he did not see Tracey. Then he caught sight of her and stopped dead in his tracks. Then, moving quickly to her, he asked, "Tracey, what you doing here? Your mother is all right?"

Tracey burst into tears. Sobs shook her so much that her father had to hold her up. He put her into the truck and quieted her crying so she could speak.

"Daddy, you can't leave us. Mother going crazy. She get small and she don't eat. She just crying all day. I come home from country today and meet her lying down on my bed, just crying. She don't eat all day. Daddy, why you leave us?"

Samuel started to cry too. "I coming home, Tracey. I coming home. I can't live without Cintie either. Is just that she so miserable all the time. She always cursing me. I just get fed up."

Tracey hugged him. "You going leave the woman house?"

Samuel hung his head. "Chile, I miss you and Cintie. This woman is not a woman to live wid. She don't want to live with no man and she don't want no man live with her. Besides, she don't like to wash and she can't cook. She fungie lumpy, lumpy, she cook rice like pap and she prefer to live by she-self."

Suddenly they both laughed. He went inside the house and came out with the battered suitcase filled with his clothes and his undershorts. He could not wait to hear Cintie's hands going croops, croops, croops, washing, washing, washing. He could not wait to see her moving about the yard, cooking, cooking, cooking. He could not wait to taste her food, eating, eating, eating.

Miss Amoury's Bathwater

Nurse Hannah stood looking at the sleeping Miss Amoury as she lay on her bed. Her thin and wasted body wore clean clothes, and Nurse Hannah thought it looked as if somebody was taking good care of her. She said out-loud, 'though she was quite alone with Miss Amoury: "I wonder is who looking after her? Her clothes clean-clean."

She was not sure that Miss Amoury was alive, for her breathing was indiscernible. She bent over the old woman and just then, the gaunt, frail body moved, and a thin sigh escaped the dry, cracked lips.

Miss Amoury was very much alive.

Nurse Hannah sat heavily in the chair next to the bed, grateful for its convenient proximity to her behind. She was definitely getting too old for this home practitioner business, she thought. "Too old or too fat—take you pick," she muttered to herself. "I'm both."

She smiled ruefully. "You definitely getting old, you talking to youself now," she said and smiled at her private conversation with herself.

Miss Amoury's little house had such a putrid smell that Nurse Hannah expected to see rotting food, even a dead rat, drying up in the corner; but nothing could be seen, so she got up to investigate more fully. The house looked very clean and there was no food left out. Nurse Hannah thought it looked as if Miss Amoury ate only lettuce, tomatoes, tinned salmon, bread, sardines, onions, eggs, cucumber, cheese and sliced sausage. She saw their remains in Miss Amoury's rubbish bin and in her cupboards.

The smell persisted, but by now Nurse Hannah's nostrils were becoming quite accustomed to it. She sat in the one chair in the little house and looked around, still trying to determine the source of the bad smell. It was the kind of smell that came from decaying vegetables or something mossy. Then suddenly she came upon the source under the foot of Miss Amoury's bed: a bath pan of fermenting green water.

Nurse Hannah woke up Miss Amoury and asked her what was fermenting in the bath pan. At first Miss Amoury would not answer. It was only after much prompting that she told the nurse a most wondrous tale.

First she begged Nurse Hannah to please pull the bath pan from under her bed. "I was having it hard. I couldn't get nothing at all done for me, not even to pay a light bill. You see how dey cut off de light?" Nurse Hannah nodded, although she wondered how Miss Amoury expected her to notice this when it was full sunlight.

Miss Amoury's voice gained strength as she continued, "I start to feel weak and have stomach pains, so I send a message to my son, but I understand he in jail again. So I had was to do something for meself. I send a message to a man name Piggott who does bathe people to change de way tings going." She paused, coughed weakly and looked sheepishly at Nurse Hannah.

Nurse Hannah was trying her best to keep a straight face at the thought of Miss Amoury's body being bathed by a burly man like Piggott. She knew him to be a big man, thickset and muscular. She had no doubt that Piggott was an obeah man— everyone said so, and there were some foolish women who allowed him to bathe them. The town joked that one day, when Piggott was supposed to be bathing some young woman to help her change the way her life was going, her boyfriend came home and caught them in bed together. People said that Piggott ran for his life from the house, naked as he was born.

"So what happen?" Nurse Hannah asked. She tried to keep an unbiased tone in her voice as she questioned Miss Amoury. "What you do?"

Miss Amoury was impatient. "I tell you I send for de man!" She was embarrassed enough telling the story without Nurse Hannah questioning her so closely. Now shy of telling the rest of the story, she said "choopse" to frighten off Nurse Hannah and make her feel humble. But Miss Amoury had bargained without Nurse Hannah's persistence. She left the story to rest for the moment. She was used to looking after old women like Miss Amoury and used to Miss Amoury too.

She pottered around the little house, straightening things here and there. She asked Miss Amoury if there was anything she could get for her from the nearby shop, and Miss Amoury asked for a loaf of bread. Nurse Hannah returned from the store and cut the bread in half to make a sandwich for Miss Amoury. She had also bought a tin of sardines, a tomato and an onion. She put some of the sardines, a few slices of the tomato and a thin slice of the onion on the bread and served it to Miss Amoury. Then she made the old woman some brebrige and sat again on the chair next to the bed.

Nurse Hannah fixed an eye on Miss Amoury and asked, "Did de man come, Miss Amoury?" The old woman could go more than one round. Me not telling her no more, she said to herself. But under Nurse Hannah's fixed eye she felt compelled to answer. She decided she would answer just this question and no other.

"Yes, he come! 'Ent I tell you I send for him? Of course he come!" Miss Amoury paused again and coughed. Nurse Hannah sighed and gave her a sip of the brebrige from the cup on the little table next to the bed. Then she took the old woman's blood pressure and listened to her heartbeat. "How come you always listening to me old heart?" Miss Amoury asked her in an irritated voice.

Nurse Hannah laughed, "How come you avoiding de issue? What is in de bath pan under you bed?"

As she spoke the nurse changed the bandage and dressing on Miss Amoury's hand. Miss Amoury had told her she had burned her finger some days ago while cooking a supper of cornmeal porridge. The hot cornmeal had left the back of her hand raw. She bit her lip when the nurse's hands got close to the wound, then sighed when the soothing balm Nurse Hannah squeezed from a tube touched her hand. She looked at the nurse's stern face as she bandaged her hand. Miss Amoury knew her well enough to know she had a good heart. She decided to tell her the whole story.

Nurse Hannah registered no surprise when Miss Amoury suddenly said, "I have something private to tell you." She paused and looked at Nurse Hannah closely. Nurse Hannah said nothing, but she smiled. Her face softened as she looked at her patient.

"You can speak to me openly. I won't betray you confidence."

"Well, Nurse, the obeah man come and me tell him how me feeling and he go way and come back and bring all different kind'a bush. He put on water to boil, and meantime, he pick out certain bush and he put them in me cup. The rest'a bush, he put them in de bath pan. When de water boil up he pour some on de bush in me cup and he pour de rest on de bush in me bath pan. Meantime, he put in cold water till it cool down." She paused and Nurse Hannah gave her another sip of brebrige. Miss Amoury laid back on her pillows and fanned herself with a delicate straw fan.

"De bush water was nice smelling. And den he tell me to go in de bath pan and let de water lap up on me while I drinking de bush tea from me cup. Den he tell me dat he will have to bathe me." Miss Amoury took a deep breath and looked at Nurse Hannah.

Nurse Hannah kept a straight face. She wished that she could laugh.

Miss Amoury continued, "Well, Nurse, you know me no show me skin easy. You even did have trouble wid me dat way. But next ting me know, me jump in de bath pan in me naked skin. It was most peculiar, Nurse. Most peculiar."

Miss Amoury paused. Nurse Hannah held her counsel. The corners of her mouth twitched as she tried to picture Miss Amoury naked, with an obeah man bathing her. She had tried to give Miss Amoury a full bath many times but usually had to be content to give her a sponge bath because the old woman would not take off her flannel vest and her drawers. Nurse Hannah used to wipe one foot at a time because Miss Amoury would caution her, "Don't take off me two socks one time!" When Nurse Hannah asked her why not she answered, "Me never like to strip down everything one time, just so." So Nurse Hannah would wipe one foot, put the sock back on it and then wipe the other foot.

Some time ago, Miss Amoury had told Nurse Hannah that her husband, now dead, never saw her naked, and they had been married for thirty-eight years. When Miss Amoury was pregnant with her first child she went into labour while taking a bath, and when she cried out, her husband came running from outside. She stopped him at the door, telling him that she was naked and he could not come in.

"Nurse! Nurse! That man bathe me so gentle; it was nice!" Nurse Hannah looked at Miss Amoury as if she were a complete stranger. She murmured under her breath, "How this could have happened?"

"Nurse! When I tell you gentle, you know, Nurse, I mean gentle. De man take a cloth—" here Miss Amoury paused, reached over to her table and took a cloth from her Bible. "See it here. He leave it with me at my request."

Nurse Hannah smiled openly now. She shook her head, "You must be crazy. How you could make dis man bathe you, Miss Amoury?" Then she asked half-seriously, "You don't fraid he ask you for wife?"

Miss Amoury laughed and made a tut-tut sound. She wagged her head at Nurse Hannah. "Ask me for wife, Nurse? You crazy, Nurse? That is a serious man. He don't mean any freshness."

When she spoke again, her voice contained some hurt. "Nurse, I am a old woman. What man would do such a ting? You don't understand. This man help me. He bathe me so gentle with dis cloth, I feel like a new-born baby. Pure and clean.

Then he tell me to throw 'way the water at the crossroads. And I was to throw two pennies with it."

Nurse Hannah looked at her curiously, "Well, why you still have it under you bed?" Miss Amoury was decidedly upset now. She looked slyly at Nurse Hannah.

"Ah don't have nobody to ask to do such a ting for me," she said.

"Don't look at me!" Nurse Hannah said sharply.

"But Nurse," Miss Amoury's voice was pleading, "Nurse, that's why I so sick. I suppose to throw 'way de water—otherwise I not going get better." She was very agitated, and the excitement made her cough. When she caught her breath she continued excitedly, "One ting though, Nurse, when I throw out de water, if anybody take up de pennies dat in it, dey will get whatever ailing me."

At last Nurse Hannah felt that she could laugh openly. She threw back her head and laughed and laughed. "What? Who tell you that Miss Amoury, de obeah man?" As Miss Amoury nodded Nurse Hannah kept laughing. She finally paused long enough to say, "I will throw 'way de water for you."

Miss Amoury let out a big breath. "Praise be to God," she said.

Nurse Hannah shook a finger at her, "I wouldn't include God in this if I was you," she said, but she smiled at the old woman.

Encouraged by Nurse Hannah's smile, Miss Amoury confided, "Nurse, you don't believe so you don't understand how it really work, you know. Me sick-sick; sicker than before since me sleeping with that bath pan of bad water under the foot of the bed." She took a deep breath and another sip of brebrige.

When Miss Amoury resumed there was an unmistakable

sadness in her voice, "First, Nurse, de obeah man bathe me and leave de water in the middle of me house. He say to me that he not suppose to throw it 'way for me. I must get some unconcerned person to do dat for me. Well, you know me friend Mavis who does come and do little tings for me?"

Nurse Hannah nodded. She knew Mavis well, for she had to ask her to run some errands for Miss Amoury from time to time. Miss Amoury's voice was sad and hurt as she spoke of Mavis. "Nurse, dat woman was such a pretender. Is she set jumbie on me in de first place, but I didn't believe it until I see it wid me own two eyes." She sat up higher in the bed now, gaining strength from the memory of Mavis's betrayal. "Ah send to call Mavis, Nurse, and she come quick-quick, as if she really concern 'bout me, you know?" Nurse Hannah nodded. She had always found that whenever she approached Mavis to do chores for Miss Amoury she always acted fast.

Miss Amoury continued, "Well, Nurse, nothing 'tall go so. That woman is a traitor. She envy me and she evil. When she come I say to her, 'Mavis, I did get a bush bath and the person that do it say I must do so-and-so with de water.' You understand, Nurse, I explain everything to her, very particular."

Again Nurse Hannah nodded, making sounds of encouragement in her throat. She knew that Mavis was the only person Miss Amoury trusted. Miss Amoury sighed. "Nurse, I also tell her someting I didn't tell you yet, that is about de water itself. De obeah man did tell me that when de person throw 'way de water, they must not step in it neither. In fact anybody who pass by that water must not walk in it because they will get my sickness too. Everybody know 'bout these tings. You an'all must-be hear 'bout these tings, Nurse?"

Indeed. Although Nurse Hannah did not believe in obeah she always made sure she did not walk in any water she saw thrown at a crossroads. She said, "Oh, yes, yes, I hear about these tings all the time."

Miss Amoury was pleased to see her story corroborated. "Well, Nurse, I was feeling good after de obeah man bathe me. I mean, I wasn't to perfection, but I was making out."

Nurse Hannah said, "Yes, that's how you were when I last saw you. That's why I was surprised to meet you so down, so quickly."

"Ah-h-h!" Miss Amoury exclaimed, excited at the nurse's confirmation of her deterioration. "Ah, Nurse, is true for true! There you are! I an all want to know why that happen! But hear how it go—hear how it go. That evil woman who suppose to be me friend—she come and I explain everything to her and ask her, 'Mavis, you could empty the bath pan for me at cross-roads?'"

Miss Amoury lay back on her pillow, exhausted from the exertion of talking. When she spoke again her voice was less agitated. "You know what she tell me, Nurse? Me who does do so much for that woman, me who does give her money for her grandchildren all de time, me who does give her what little food I have, me who does always give her any piece'a clothes that me children and dem send me from New York? You know what she tell me?"

Nurse Hannah shook her head. She knew how good Miss Amoury had been to Mavis. Throughout the old woman's litany of the things she had done for Mavis, Nurse Hannah had nodded and said "mmm hmm" from time to time. She asked, "What she tell you? She say she not doing it?"

Miss Amoury nodded. "Yes. She say that she have a back problem and she can't lift up no bath-pan. Well, I know that was not true, but I say well, grant her that; grant her de back problem. So I say to her, 'Well, what about Ronald'—you know him, Nurse. Dat is de man she does keep—'You tink you could ask him to do it?'" Miss Amoury's breathing was short now.

"Well, Nurse, Mavis tell me say her man is too busy to do dhose tings. And so saying, she lean down with de same bad back she say she have and she heft de bath pan, she one, and she push it under me bed."

Nurse Hannah was now intrigued but also alarmed about Miss Amoury's breathing. By now she was almost gasping from the effort it took her to speak. Nurse Hannah leaned towards her and asked, "You sure you're all right? You want anything? You looking so weak...."

Miss Amoury shook her head, "Is de water, Nurse. It killing me. I study on it and I realize that Mavis take de opportunity to push that bath pan under my bed. When she do it I say to her, 'Why you push it under my bed?' She look sheepish and she say, 'Well, I put it out of you way.' So then I study on it and I say, 'But if it not to walk in how I going sleep over it? You better pull it back out, Mavis.'

"She never do it, Nurse. She say dis and she say dat, but all de say she say, she never move that bath pan back out from under me bed. And I telling you, Nurse, from that moment I can hardly leave me bed, just to go on the 'tensil to go toilet. That boy for Fred does come to see me every day and do little things for me, but I couldn't ask him to handle me bath pan. For one thing he little and for another, that's not right, not for a little boy like that."

Miss Amoury breathed lightly now, her eyes closed. Nurse Hannah took away the brebrige cup and was preparing to leave when she heard her voice again. She turned back to the bed. "Nurse, I getting me strength back. I can feel it inside. Thank you."

Nurse Hannah shushed her. "You stay quiet now and get some rest. I will get somebody to help me to lift the bath pan outside," she promised.

When she got back to the clinic Nurse Hannah made a note in her file on Miss Amoury. She wrote, "Recovering nicely." She made no mention of the obeah man and the bush bath, nor did she write anything about going back to remove the bath pan. She was not going to risk the teasing of the other nurses who already considered her too indulgent of her patients. She left the clinic after she had put away her files and then went walking down the street. Finally she saw the person she needed—a young man talking with his friends outside a grocery store. She called to him and when he came over explained what she needed of him. He agreed willingly. Nurse Hannah had helped his mother to bring him into this world, and he would have done anything for her.

The young man and the nurse set off for Miss Amoury's house. When they entered the house Nurse Hannah was surprised to see Miss Amoury sitting at her little table, eating the other half of her bread and looking quite bright. "You get up already?" she asked.

Miss Amoury said, "You see what I tell you, Nurse? Is because de bath pan move from under me bed. I start get better right away."

Nurse Hannah was skeptical, but she would do what Miss Amoury wanted. She instructed the young man and together they lifted the fermenting bath pan and walked it to the crossroads. As they were walking out of the house Miss Amoury's caution rang in the nurse's ears. "Mind you don't step in the water and don't take up them pennies!"

They tipped the bath pan on its side and before Nurse Hannah could do anything about it, the water ran under their feet. Just then a woman standing nearby said, "Nurse, take great care. Might as well you and the young man go arrange you own bush bath right now cause all you walk in Miss Amoury bathwater. You going have her pain, Nurse. And seeing as how I hear say how that water sitting long-long time in Miss Amoury house it going be worse, Nurse."

Nurse Hannah turned to reply, and when she turned back around, she was just in time to see the young man rising from a stooping position. Nurse Hannah's voice was sharp. "What you have there?" His reply made her feel quite faint. "The two pennies that drop out of de water," he said, opening his hand to show her the coins.

Nurse Hannah sighed and said to him sharply, "Throw them back!" Then more kindly she told him, "If you get sick, send somebody to find me at the clinic." Then she gave him a dollar for helping her.

By the time Nurse Hannah reached home she could hardly walk. Her stomach ached. She got into bed, but not before sending her brother with a message asking Miss Amoury to find Piggott, the obeah man.

Before she fainted away from the pain she wondered how she would explain this to the young man who had so kindly helped her to throw out Miss Amoury's bathwater. She knew that he, too, would soon need Piggott's services.

On the Gallery

It was not as if Merine had ever really liked the way things were done in her mother's home. It was more a case of not knowing any other way. She had always seen her mother as a very uncreative woman and a rather lazy one at that, but without realising it, Merine had found herself running things in the same haphazard, sometimes chaotic, way.

The dishes, for instance: she always left them until the next day. Every time she found herself standing over a large stack of dishes she would promise herself that she would not let it happen again. A week or so would go by and she would find herself standing over a full sink, remembering that it was only when she and her sister Faye became big enough to wash the dishes that they stopped piling up in the sink.

Then the chore became theirs, and their mother announced that dishes should not be left in the sink overnight. Their father agreed with her. That's another thing I don't like about my mother's style, Merine thought irritably. The way she never asks Papa Roy to help with things around the house, and the way she has of getting him to agree with her about everything.

Merine sighed in exasperation as she remembered that as a child she and her sister had had to do all the housework, even picking up the clothes their father dropped on the floor. Her mother would manoeuvre to have things her way, and Papa Roy would let her do whatever she wanted. Even now, before Merine could tell him about a quarrel she had going with her mother, she would find her father had already been briefed. Then there would be no point in telling him her side of it because he always believed her mother. It seemed to Merine that the way he worshipped her mother was like the way people worshipped God.

When she was a teenager Merine had looked at her father with pity because her mother treated him very badly. Her mother had an affair with a younger man who used to come and visit her every night. Everyone in the neighbourhood and in the family laughed about how her father seemed quite happy. He appeared to be oblivious to his wife stepping out on him. Papa Roy had known, but he used to put up a brave front to everybody. Only Merine knew that it was a false front.

When Merine and her sister went to bed, the young man would come and visit her mother. Bold as brass he would sit in the living room. Or sometimes the two of them would sit on the gallery and talk until late at night. By then Merine's father would have come home from visiting his friends and gone to bed. Her mother would not come inside until an hour or two later. Merine and Faye went to bed at eight o'clock. Faye would fall asleep right away, but Merine would lie awake, listening for Papa Roy to come home.

First she would hear his steps. Then he would say good evening in a tight little voice. He's vex, Merine would think, he's vex because mother on the gallery with the man.

She would hear Papa Roy get a sweet drink from the fridge and say "aahh" after he drank it in one long, long swallow.

Merine would listen as her father went to the toilet and made a long, long pee as if he had been holding it in the whole night. Then he would scrub his teeth and gargle loudly, making an exaggerated sound as he spat out the water. In the meantime Merine would also hear her mother's soft, low voice out on the gallery. She never heard the young man's voice clearly. He spoke in a soft murmur that did not carry to her bedroom.

Next her father would go into his bedroom, and Merine would hear the bed creak as he sat on it, taking off first one shoe, letting it go with a thump onto the floor, and then taking the sock off his shoeless foot before he untied the other shoe. She knew that he had not loosened both lacings at the same time because there was always a long pause after the first shoe thumped to the floor. She thought it peculiar of Papa Roy, and she hugged that peculiarity close to herself. Knowing about the shoes made her feel that she knew Papa Roy better than anyone else could. She loved him best and it was right that she knew him best.

After her father had finished taking off his shoes and socks, Merine would listen as the bed creaked again when he stood up to take off his clothes. Merine would lie in the bed next to Faye, and with her head against the thin partition she would listen to the rustling of his clothes as he hung them up on the nail on the door. She would imagine him putting on his pajamas. She knew that Papa Roy got enjoyment from sleeping in pajamas. He had them made by Miss Winnie, who also sewed for his sister, and he would order another pair as soon as one of his two pairs wore out.

She smiled now. He really liked the pajamas. He liked socks, too, and he liked clean floors. He used to scrub the floors of their little house every Saturday. Sometimes Merine's mother would say, "Why you have to scrub de floor? Nothing wrong wid it, it clean."

And Papa Roy would reply, "I like it to be really clean." He would ignore her, "choopse" in disapproval, then continue to scrub the floor until the wood was so clean that Merine supposed she could eat her food from it because it was even cleaner than the table.

Today Merine remembered how Papa Roy had to defend his love of pajamas just as he had to defend his clean floors. Whenever he told her mother he was ordering a new pair of pajamas from Miss Winnie, she used to say, "Again? You going hospital? Only sick people does wear so much pajamas."

Merine remembered, too, how she used to picture him in her mind in the next room in his pajamas while her mother's low voice would talk on into the night to a man who did not belong in the house. Her voice would drop lower, grow softer after Papa Roy went to bed, as if to hide from him what she was saying. Merine would lie in bed, secure in the knowledge that Papa Roy was home in bed right next to her room and that soon he would be sleeping and dreaming, and so would she. She would hear him get into bed, and she felt sure that the bed creaked wearily, but she was sure, too, that the bed was as happy to have her father home as she was. She was sure as well that the crickets chirped more loudly and lustily after Papa Roy came home, their wings a frenzied welcoming chorus.

Her mother's voice would mumble on out on the gallery. She would hear her laugh, a deep, throaty chuckle full of life. She had not heard her mother laugh like that with anyone except the young man. Right after she laughed, Papa Roy would sigh loudly and deeply. It was a sad, sad, sigh—not at all the sigh he would make when he sat out on the gallery with his wife.

The times that her mother and father sat together on the gallery were so rare that Merine could no longer remember what those happy sighs were like, but she did remember watching Papa Roy smile and pat her mother's hand. Then he would sigh as if he were saying, "This is my beloved wife in whom I am well pleased," just the way God had talked about His beloved Son. When she heard her Sunday School teacher read those words she had wished that she could hear her mother say "beloved daughter." She knew that her father loved her because he always said nice things to her: "Merine, you such a bright girl, I really proud of you," and "Merine, you so nice, chile." But her mother never spoke to her except to criticise her.

She wondered sometimes if everybody thought about parents the way she did and if her father realised that she knew so much about him and how he felt about her mother. He loved her mother so much that Merine thought he did not realise what a terrible person she was.

Merine believed that even when he felt sad at night he did not think that his wife was so bad, just sad that she was not paying him any attention. Merine felt so sorry for poor Papa Roy.

After Papa Roy had sighed and shifted in his bed, Merine would feel the tears roll down her face. She could feel his sadness. Even though there was a partition between them, she was sure she could hear his heart beat.

Her sister Faye was so concerned about herself that she never seemed to care deeply about anything or anybody, not even Merine. She did not feel any malice towards her; that's just the way Faye was. There were times when Merine thought maybe Papa Roy loved her more than he loved Faye, but she could not be really sure. He was never unkind to Faye; he just seemed to pay more attention to Merine. Maybe Faye was so wrapped up in herself that it was difficult for anybody to pay her any attention. There were times when she thought that Faye was too simple to have the serious thoughts Merine troubled herself about every day. It seemed to her, though, that Faye was much happier than she was and she envied her that happiness even now.

Merine would continue listening to her mother's low talking and laughing with her man-friend on the gallery. Sometimes Merine would doze off and jerk awake with such a start that Faye, sound asleep beside her, would come half awake. Faye would mumble and turn over, blissfully unaware that Merine was trying to stay awake to eavesdrop. For Merine there could be no sleep until her mother went to the bedroom and got into bed beside her father. Merine would listen to him toss and turn on the creaking bed and she would know that he, too, had listened to her mother's throaty laugh and soft talk. She longed to comfort him but knew that she could never let him know what she had heard, let alone that she had understood.

Finally Merine would hear her mother call out good night. She imagined her mother standing on the gallery, watching the young man walk down the street, waiting until he reached the corner before she called out to him. Only then would she come into the house and close and lock the front door.

Her mother, too, had a pattern for the way she prepared for bed. She would go to the fridge and get herself a sweet drink. Next she would wash out the glass she had used. Then she washed her face and scrubbed her teeth. Merine knew that because she heard her make the sound she always made with her mouth when she passed her hand down over it—a loud, whooshing sound. Then she would take some of the water into her mouth, and spitting it out, she would begin to scrub her teeth. She was louder than Papa Roy and seemed not to care that everyone else in the house was in bed trying to sleep. She would sometimes sing part of a hymn that Merine had heard her sing ever since Merine was a little, little girl.

It was such a pretty hymn that Merine used to tell herself she must make sure that they sang that hymn at her mother's funeral. It had a really pretty tune and the words were nice too. Sometimes Merine would hum a line from it when she was bathing: *And may there be no mourning at the barge, when I put out to sea.*

All the same, she would sometimes ask Jesus, "Why You let mother sing this beautiful hymn when she was so bad to Papa Roy?" She had blamed Jesus, too, for allowing her mother and Faye to be so much happier than her and Papa Roy. She thought that the least He could have done was to zap her mother with a bolt of lightning for being so bad to her father.

Merine sat in her living room feeling quite unhappy with herself. Now she was a mother and she saw herself being the same kind of woman that her mother had been and she did not like it one bit. Today she would change things, make them different, she told herself. Today she would not behave like her mother; she would take stock of things and change to become a person she could be proud of. She would not let the chaos continue.

She did not really know what to do, but she was determined that things would be different. She thought of her father, of how her mother had had a lover all those years, of her own life. She looked up at the picture of her husband on the little shelf over the television set. He was so handsome and so sweet, but she found herself hurting him all the time, just the way her mother had hurt her father.

She thought of her lover, suave, debonair and too handsome, serving no real purpose in her life. She felt sick to her stomach at the thought of it all. For at least two years she had been trying to convince herself that she was not like her mother. But today there was no doubt in her mind that she was very much like her mother, much more so than Faye, who was too full of herself to be like anyone else. Faye had managed to grow up without noticing her mother enough to pick up any of her habits.

Merine and her mother hardly discussed anything. The few conversations they had still rang in Merine's ears, though some of them had taken place four or five years ago. Mostly, though they never said so, they fought for her father's attention. He had always favoured Merine over Faye, her mother said, and this had made her angry. She was also angry and jealous that he bought things for Merine every time he got paid and would remind him, as Merine watched him grind his teeth, that he had two daughters and a wife. She was only a little girl at the time and never really understood what was going on. Her child's mind had simply registered that her mother was preventing the one person who loved her from showing her that love.

One day Merine had heard herself attacking her husband

for no reason. As she watched her husband grind his teeth she felt so sorry, but she did not know how to make up to him. She had no experience in asking for forgiveness, and to apologise was to admit that she had lost.

Now that Merine was turning forty she thought that maybe the phrase "life begins at forty" was not so trite after all. Maybe she would strike some new beginning. Whenever she went home to visit her parents she started to listen to her mother intently. And she started listening to herself too. She found many similarities and few differences. Merine wanted to be softer, gentler—more like the little girl who used to listen to her father going to bed and who used to feel so sorry for him as he waited tossing and turning for her mother to come to bed that she used to cry herself to sleep. She liked that little girl, was proud of her.

As her fortieth birthday drew closer, she sought out her father more and more. She did not plan it but found that there were days that she needed to be near him, see the welcome in his big, light-brown eyes. Her father had "pussy eyes," like Merine's, and like Merine's, his eyes stood out in his dark skin. Some days Merine watched her father gazing at her mother with a kind of puzzled wonder, as if he questioned how he came to be so in love with her or how he had been so lucky to have her. Whenever her mother would notice him looking at her, she would snap, "Take you pussy-eye off me."

Merine used to flinch when her mother spoke like that to her father, and then she would flinch on her own behalf as her mother would look from father to daughter.

Sometimes Merine would wonder if she belonged to her mother. Maybe she just had Faye, she would think. But then she would look at her mother's smile and see her own, look at her toes and see her mother's toes, look at how her cheeks dimpled when she bit in her lips, and she would know that she was her mother's daughter. Faye had her mother's eyes and that was all.

When Merine was honest with herself she had to admit that she admired some things about her mother, but it was mixed with a loathing that prevented her from being able to feel good about what she admired. When she was a little girl she used to love to watch her mother bathe, and she would hope that that was what her body would be like when she grew up. She had never seen a more beautiful person. Merine never let her mother know that she watched her bathe because she knew that her mother would make her stop.

There was only a face-basin and a toilet in the house, so everyone bathed out in the fenced-in yard. Merine's father had put up a little shed. It did not have a door, but you could bathe in it without anybody seeing you, unless they made an effort. Sitting out on the big stone heap in the yard, Merine would pretend that she was reading. Waiting until she heard the water splashing, she would slowly raise her head to watch her mother as she washed.

Merine felt sure now that her mother had loved her body. She would wash her private parts, as she called them, several times. Next she would wash the long hair under her arms—hair that was a different colour and texture from the hair on her head but that matched her other body hair. Then she would take a wash cloth and stretch to wash her back thoroughly. Sometimes she would sing as she washed her arms and legs, raising her head to reach a high note. Then she would wash each breast carefully as if it hurt, then raise each one to clean the place where her breasts rested above her belly.

One day Merine was so intently watching her mother bathe that she did not hear her father come into the yard. When he spoke to her she jumped and dropped her book. "Chile, go and play!" he said to her sharply, and she ran off feeling very embarrassed. He never said anything to her about the incident, but one day when she was fifteen years old he asked her if she liked boys. "No," she shook her head. Her father had looked very concerned. After that Merine noticed that he looked worriedly at her from time to time, but she did not understand his concern until she was a full-grown woman. Soon after that, he seemed to forget the incident because he was too unhappy about her mother's new boyfriend to think about anything else.

Merine would be in bed when the new boyfriend arrived so she never saw him. She had seen the old boyfriend once, when she and Faye were at Dicky Lake's shop picking up the groceries. They saw their mother talking to a man and heard him say, "See you later, maybe around eight o'clock." Merine had figured out that he must be the man that came to their house every night. Her mother had been flustered and had hustled them out of the store. Now there was a new man and Merine could tell that Papa Roy was upset.

He would come in after she had gone to bed, but he did not have a sweet drink, scrub his teeth and go to bed, tossing and turning until her mother came into the bedroom. Instead he started to sit in the living room for awhile. On the third night he went back out and did not return until long after the man left. On the fourth night Papa Roy did not come home after work. Merine searched her parents' faces closely for the next three days and could see differences but nothing she could put her finger on right away.

Her mother sang more and her father drank more rum than usual, but nothing pointed to the cause for the change in his routine. She did notice that her Papa Roy no longer said "Aahh" after tossing off his drinks of rum and water, but that did not tell her anything much.

On the fourth night, when Papa Roy did not come home after work, her mother looked very worried. Merine decided that she would have to find out what was happening. She got out of bed and went into the living room and sat quietly listening to her mother's soft conversation with the man on the gallery. From behind the nylon curtains at the window she peeped out on the gallery for a good look at the man. What a shock Merine got when she saw not the man they had seen in Dicky Lake's store but a different man altogether.

This man was light-skinned and young. He had curly hair, just like the doll that her aunt had sent for her from New York, and he had it parted to the side and slicked down. He did not look Antiguan to Merine. He looked Dominican or St. Lucian to her, just like her friend Wilhemina, who was from Dominica. Just then Papa Roy had come home and caught Merine peeping out of the curtain. He had opened the unlocked door very abruptly, and Merine had been so absorbed that she had not heard his footsteps. He had not said his usual good evening either, but it was only later, when she was lying in bed, that she realised that. "Papa Roy really vex, he didn't even tell them good evening," she mumbled into her pillow.

Papa Roy spoke to Merine very sharply when he caught her out of bed, and she was ashamed at being caught peeping at her mother. She knew he would not tell her mother about it and that his anger was not aimed at her. "Girl, what you doing out of you bed?" Papa Roy did not speak loudly, but his tone was gruff. "Is late," he continued. "Just go back to bed and go sleep."

She hastily went back to her bedroom and had to be content with listening through the thin wall. She could hear her father watching television in the living room, while her mother entertained her friend on the gallery. Sometimes she heard Papa Roy get up and go to the fridge or the bathroom and she knew he must have been out drinking with his friends because that was the only time he used the bathroom so often. Then she heard him go to bed as her mother called goodbye to her friend.

The more time she spent with her father the more she discovered she still saw him through a child's eyes. She still liked what she saw. Her father was still the gentlest and most loving of souls and she still loved him best. He seemed to be very happy that she was seeking him out. Whenever his eyes lit up as he looked at her she would feel the peace and warmth she remembered feeling as a child. He had the spirit that she wanted to have herself.

Merine's visits to her father were usually in the early evening. Sometimes they sat on the gallery and watched people walk up or down the street. Other times he would tell her about his life, and there were times when they would be disrupted by her mother's noisy arrival. These days her mother visited a close woman friend every evening. Merine thought her mother was too old to have a lover and so had found another distraction to keep her from being around Papa Roy. She would arrive home, displeased, if not downright annoyed, to see Merine and her father sitting peacefully talking. "You two not tired talking?" or, "Mmm, mmm. What all you have to talk 'bout so?" Merine always beat a quick retreat, for she was determined not to quarrel with her mother.

Merine and her father had a lot to talk about, although some days when she visited they did not speak very much at all, just sat comfortably together. But there were days they really talked: about how Merine felt about becoming forty, about how life had gone for her and for him. They never talked about his relationship with her mother. It was what she most wanted to talk about because she felt that understanding it would help her to understand herself. If nothing else she wanted to understand why she was so much like her mother and she wanted to change the way she was with men.

One day her father was sitting with her on the gallery picking his teeth with a matchstick while Merine sipped a sweet drink. A man and woman walked up the street. They watched the couple idly as Merine wondered who they were. Now that she had grown up and moved away there were many people who passed on the street that she did not know at all. She had turned to her father to ask him about the couple as he said to her, "You know dose people dere?" Merine shook her head.

"The man is a Vincentian," he said. "He come to Antigua to work at de oil refinery. The woman is from Cedargrove and de man like her as soon as he meet her and widdin a short time he married to her. All went well for awhile, den de woman start to have other men and dey does go to de house and visit her at nighttime, right under de husband nose."

As he continued to tell her about how the man's wife had been disrespectful to him by allowing her men to visit her in his house it occurred to Merine that he was describing his wife.

She looked at him carefully out of the corners of her eyes.

"You know you mother do de same thing to me?" Merine was too stunned by the suddenness of the question to do more than nod. Suddenly she felt very close to tears. Her father picked his teeth for awhile, watching the couple as they walked up the street.

"It was a hard time in my life, chile." The last time Merine remembered him calling her that was when his mother died and Merine had been unable to stop crying. It was only a few years ago, but she had felt like a little child and a silly one at that because she had not known her grandmother well. She was from Jennings and had refused to come to town for the last ten years of her life. Merine's mother had not liked her very much, leaving it to Papa Roy to make sure that he took Merine to visit his mother every Christmas and every harvest.

He never took Faye, though Merine used to beg him to take her with them. "She too small," he would say, and she used to know that he was lying, but she could never understand why he would lie about it. Faye neither cared nor even noticed she was being excluded.

Merine had cried out of pity for her father. His mournful face was all it took for her to feel sad. Then he had stroked her hand and called her chile. She had wondered how he was going to spend his Saturdays. While his mother was alive he spent every Saturday out in Jennings, visiting her and taking care of any heavy work that needed doing.

Now he picked his teeth and called her chile. He seemed to brace himself to continue: "I determined wid God's help to wait for you mother to come to she senses. I love her, you know, and when you love somebody, you don't just love dem when dey good. You love dem all de time."

He paused again. Merine could not speak. Then he said, "In the end is I who win all the battle. You mother and them men continue and continue. I talk to her serious and show her that the lessons she setting her daughters—those was bad lessons. I not response for her soul, but I response for her guiding. I older than she, and besides, I stronger than she."

Merine was surprised at this last statement because she had always seen her mother as the stronger one, just as she saw herself as the stronger person in the relationship with her husband. She asked her father, "How you mean you stronger than mother?"

He smiled, and it was a smile filled with smug satisfaction. Merine thought that at that moment her father looked powerful and all-seeing.

"I know life. I see life and I watch it and I live it. You mother don't even know what life 'bout. She use to tink dat she give me a six for a nine. Is like when you girls was little: you do someting and you feel me and you mother don't know you do de ting. Like de day ah catch you watching you mother bathe. You did feel dat you was getting away wid pretending dat you reading and you watching you mother bathe all de time. Well, you mother did know and I did know 'cause she tell me. That day ah catch you was the first time I see you doing it, but you mother did know every single time you do it and she used to laugh at it. I didn't like it so ah stop you."

He paused. When her father spoke again Merine noticed the sadness in his voice. "Well, chile, you mother was like that. Like a little girl, doing the ting and feeling that she get 'way with it. I only now see she begin to respect she-self and stop harbour man round her. And now ah let her know that ah did always know, but when I married to her I married to her for better or for worse."

He paused to spit out bits of food that he had been picking from his teeth. He took a deep breath and said, "Ah see de worse, chile, now I having de better part," and then he laughed.

Merine laughed, too, although she did so a bit shakily; she was moved by her father's openness. She had never before heard him say so much at once. After that day, he talked to her more openly, no longer shy with her, as if he had always known that she had pitied him for the humiliation her mother had caused him.

Another day as they sat on the gallery talking, he turned to her and said, as if continuing that first conversation about her mother, "She did much more than you realise, you know, chile."

"How you mean Papa Roy?" He looked at her carefully, and after a long pause said flatly, "You know, chile, Faye is only you half-sister. You mother did love that particular man, I think. She used to go crazy whenever I touch her during the time. I was making up me mind to lose her, but I pray every day that she stay because I know that she was de woman I suppose to marry and honour. And besides, that man didn't mean her no good—he was a real louse."

He paused and brushed a hand across his eyes. Merine

knew that her own eyes were full of tears. She did not blink for she did not want them to fall.

Papa Roy continued, "I look at her and I know she is de only person for me; you just know these things, chile. Me mother always say: 'Is you one can choose you bed and is you one have to lie in it.'"

Merine nodded wordlessly. She knew what he meant. She had felt herself drawn to her husband as if with a seine net. Finally, she stated almost to herself, "That's why you always prefer me to Faye, Papa Roy."

Her father looked at her with surprise, "You did notice that?" Merine nodded, remembering how her mother complained that he did not pay the same attention to Faye.

Suddenly Merine realised another awful truth. "You never tell Mother that you know?"

Her father shook his head, "No, as I explain to you, you mother is like you and Faye was when you was children. She feel she get away with the deeds she do and I had to wait till she grow up and come big woman before I tell her the tings I know and the understanding I have."

Merine stared at him then heard him speak as if from a distance. "She know now, but in dose days, when you was little, she was trying to pass off the chile as mine. Well of a truth, I was trying to accept Faye, too, but it was hard."

Again he passed his hand across his eyes; his face looked lined and tired. His voice was almost a whisper as he said, "Faye father is a bad man. He didn't care. He had no scruple'-tall, you know. He would come to the house and whistle and Celine would tell me, 'Ah coming now, Roy. Ah getting a ride go by Urlings Village.' Next ting I know, she leave me and you and jump in dat man car. I was really de one that look after you most nights in those days. You was just a young baby, not even finish nursing yet."

Merine looked closely at her father and noticed for the first time that his shoulders stooped. It seemed to her that his grey hair was now in sharper contrast to his dark skin. She tried to imagine his life with her mother. He had married her when he was a man of thirty and she a girl of sixteen. He had grown old waiting for her to grow up. His health was failing. Merine had always thought that her father looked very young and that he had a vibrant spirit.

He looked out the window, staring fixedly at the gutter. Merine stared, too, at the green slimy water trickling into the street.

Body and Soul

The elegant woman turned the key in the lock and stepped into the house. She was young-looking, but if you looked hard at her you could see that she had long passed her thirtieth birthday and probably her fortieth. The casual observer would not notice, Dolores thought.

Her teeth flashed as she smiled or spoke; they, too, betrayed her age, for they were beginning to lose some of their thick enamel and were thinning at the edges. Otherwise they were perfectly even and white. Her mother used to look at Dolores admiringly whenever she smiled and say, "Of all my children, your teeth are the best."

Dolores had that look that comes from years of being confident. She wore a cool, crisp, business suit under a dark-coloured coat with clean, straight lines. She carried a slim briefcase and black, unlined gloves—leather gloves that she never wore but carried in the same hand as the briefcase. She was the picture of elegance and certainty.

She opened the door to her house and walked in with a smile on her face. She had about her the air of someone looking forward to letting her hair down. Dolores did not have any hair to speak of, however. She wore it very short in an Afro, or what she preferred to call "a natural." "Afro" was so mundane, she thought, and rang of a time and feeling that did not describe her at all. "Afro"—the hairstyle that heralded the Black Power era—was not a word Dolores wished to be a part of her image. She considered herself to be a very aware Black woman and was proud of the Black cultural revolution underway when she first came to North America.

She had not been really involved in it but had looked on. Granted, she had learned a lot from reading and thinking and from listening to some very interesting people speak. She just did not want to have her hairstyle branded as a part of a large-scale movement. But now that everyone had departed from the natural look, or the "Afro," as everyone else called it, Dolores felt smug in thinking she was making a political statement in the midst of wet curls.

Dolores sighed, happy to be home. Here she did not have to account to anyone for anything. She did not even have to answer the telephone. She could be completely herself, without worry of recrimination, or loss of face, business or friends.

The hallway was dark and she turned on the light, sighing again. When she left home in the morning it was dark, and by the time she returned home it was dark again. "I'm becoming an owl," she said aloud. "An owl who never sees the sun." As she took off her coat, she looked into the living room beyond the glass doors dividing it from the hallway.

She hung up her coat on the antique coat rack bought in a little shop she frequented on Queen Street. She went in there so often that the proprietor gave her special deals now and then on lamps and bric-a-brac. She had put down her briefcase for a moment next to the coat rack, and now she moved it into the hall closet to keep the hallway tidy. She kicked off her shoes, and holding them in one hand, she made her way to her bedroom, exhaling through her mouth as she walked up the stairs.

The upstairs was carefully done in muted pastel colours, with soft cushions in places where she might sometimes feel like lying down or just sitting with a book. The bathroom held a small love-seat at one end, next to a little table and a tall antique lamp. Dolores had the bathroom enlarged soon after she bought the house. It had always been her dream to have a bathroom into which she did not just dash, bathe and dash out. She liked being able to relax with a book in there.

Two large ferns were hanging in the bathroom, and she liked to think of them soaking up the steam from her baths. The singing of a bird in a gilded cage by the window made Dolores feel vital and energetic while she bathed every morning.

At the end of the upstairs corridor stood a library with the finest collection of Caribbean writers, English classics and a few Canadian works of which she had either read reviews or seen the authors interviewed on television. She was determined not to have trash in her library and kept the few comic books she had collected on a shelf in the walk-in closet in her bedroom. She also had one or two books by a few choice Black American writers. She did not, however, buy what everyone else read. Zora Neale Hurston was a favourite, and she delighted in having people ask who Zora was, so that she could extol her virtues as a writer, directly quoting Alice Walker without acknowledgement.

Next to the library was the spare bedroom, used as little as possible. Dolores made sure of that. House guests poked into her life and some had even stolen small items of hers. There was the time, for instance, she had given shelter to a young man, the son of an old friend. He stayed with her for two weeks and when he had gone she realised her little brass herb-pipe had gone with him. She had bought the pipe in Los Angeles on a weekend visit to her cousin and had treasured it as a memento. She had been high on herb for the entire weekend, and it always made her smile to look at the pipe.

Another time she had her nephew over for a weekend and when he had gone, one of her Caribbean novels was missing. She noticed it right away because she knew how her books looked next to each other on the shelves. She had not known which book was missing but had telephoned her nephew. When he said hello she had simply said, "I would like you to bring back the book immediately, please," and hung up the telephone. He had brought it back sheepishly within the hour. Dolores had not spoken to him. She had opened the door in answer to his timid knock, taken the book and slammed the door in his face. Dolores did not speak to that nephew for six months. Every time he telephoned her she would say, "Sorry, I'm busy right now. I'll talk to you later."

Eventually, he had stopped calling. One Sunday she was having the whole family over to dinner and had called him to invite him. A woman answered, and when he came to the telephone, she had invited him to the dinner party. "But," she told him, "don't bring that woman with you. It's only for family." He had come despite her rudeness and without his woman. The rift between them was repaired, but Dolores made a mental note that she would not invite him to stay overnight with her again.

The guest room was flanked on the other side by Dolores's bedroom. It had a vast dome-shaped skylight that dominated the roof, giving the room so much daylight that the plants hanging in one section of the room and those adorning the broad bay window were as green as if growing in a tropical rain forest. A mirror at one end of the room took over the wall. A large Benjamina tree stood against it. The bed was an antique four-poster in solid oak with ornate finishings on the posts and at the head and foot. On the floor lay large Persian rugs in muted maroon, grey, navy-blue and beige. The curtains were in a soft beige and peach and matching cushions lay scattered around the room.

At one end of the bedroom was a small love-seat, the twin of the one in the bathroom. In front of it was a long, narrow coffee table with the latest issues of *The New Yorker, Newsweek, Ebony, Essence, Time* and *Maclean's*. The bottom shelf of the coffee table held a large pictorial book on Africa, another on Prince Edward Island, and a few old copies of *The Economist, The Guardian* and *Toronto Life*.

Dolores loved her bedroom second only to her living room, but she liked her bedroom more when there was a man in it with her. There were, however, few men she allowed into her bedroom. She was less picky about the men whose bedrooms she went into. One man who had entry to Dolores's bedroom any time was Mark, the husband of one of her best friends. Their affair had been going on for eight years, and Dolores still managed a comfortable friendship with Cheryl, his wife. She felt no guilt because she felt quite confident that Cheryl did not know how to make Mark happy. On the contrary, Dolores knew that if she had met Mark first they would have had the perfect marriage. Dolores had so firmly convinced herself that she saw no need to seek Mark's confirmation.

She took off her clothes while standing in the large, walk-in closet that served as a dressing room. She hung up her suit and walked to the bed, clad only in the silk blouse she had worn under the suit. She sat on the bed, then lay back with her legs dangling over the edge. Slowly she unbuttoned her blouse as she lay there, feeling too tired even to finish undressing. She undid the buttons, but could not summon the energy to get up and take off her blouse. She wanted to have a nice hot bath but was too tired to get up and do anything about it.

She lay there in a drowsy haze, not falling asleep, just drift-ing. Suddenly she felt watched and she jumped up with a start but could see no one in the bedroom. She lay back on the bed and shook her head at her foolishness. "How could I be watched? No one's in this house. It's burglar proof and this bedroom is at least thirty feet off the ground," she said aloud. She felt the eyes again. This time she knew exactly where they were: above the skylight. She looked up and sure enough a man lay flat on the skylight, staring at her.

Dolores did not scream. She jumped up and waved her arms at him in a shooing motion. She knew he could not hear her, but she shouted at him anyway. He did not move. She went over to the bedside table and picked up the telephone. It was only then that the man began to scramble off the roof.

It was difficult for Dolores to make out his features. All she could tell the police was that he was white and seemed tall as he stretched out on her skylight. She could give them no details save a vague description of the colour of his clothes. The police promised to keep an eye on her house for the next few days and suggested that she move her bed from under the skylight. She thought that silly and although she agreed to do so she dismissed it as soon as they left.

That night Dolores slept fitfully under the skylight, waking every hour or so to see if the man had returned. She had several disturbing dreams that night; all included the man who had been spread-eagled on her skylight and all were erotic. She felt ashamed of the dreams but laughed at herself when she was awakened by a more realistic dream in which she lay sleeping and the man fell through the skylight on top of her. She woke up sweating and feeling a heavy pressure on her body, as if the man had really fallen on top of her. She looked at the clock. It was two in the morning.

She got up and went downstairs to make a cup of tea, hoping to be able to get back to sleep. By now she was worried about what shape she would be in for work in the morning. She went into the kitchen and saw that she had not cleaned it up. She had never before gone to bed until she had cleaned and put away every utensil, every piece of cutlery and every dish. The remains of the light dinner she had eaten after the police had left were still on a plate on top of the counter in the breakfast nook. She had eaten too late that night. Usually, she had dinner as early as six o'clock and no later than eight, but because of the incident she had eaten after nine o'clock. It was no wonder, she thought, that she could not sleep—her food was probably still undigested.

She still felt uneasy about the man on the skylight and was sure he was contributing to her sleeplessness. She tried to block him from her mind but found it as impossible awake as it had been asleep. She realised self-consciously that the skylight now bothered her. The skylight was the envy of every woman friend and even a couple of her men friends. One man

Dolores slept with occasionally used to prefer to come over to her place instead of having her over to his just to be under her skylight. He had never told her this, but she could tell by the way he always made sure they were centred under the skylight when they made love. She smiled now at the memory. Poor old Jeff, she thought, he would have freaked out if he had been here. Jeff is such a coward.

Jeff had known about all the years that Dolores had been Mark's mistress. One night he had met Mark at her house but had not said anything about it for three years. Then one day he told her, "You're in love with Mark and I don't stand a chance with you, Dee."

When Dolores looked surprised he had said, "Oh yes, I know. You think I'm stupid? But it doesn't matter, Dee. I don't hold it against you, you can't help it. But I need somebody who's with me and me alone." He had said a lot more, but Dolores had not heard it.

She started to put away the dinner dishes, beginning to feel more and more that she wanted to have somebody of her own, somebody whom she could have called tonight. She suddenly missed Jeff, for he was single and had doted on her. For a moment she considered calling him up and asking him to come over, but then she remembered he was serious about someone else. She did not know if he was living with her. Maybe he got married, Dolores mused. Then she smiled. No, he would have told me he was getting married.

After she finished cleaning up the kitchen she sat at the breakfast counter, sipping her tea and wondering how she was going to get through the next day at work. Her employer was a miserable man, mercenary and demanding. Dolores was sure that they were the most watched employees in Toronto. It was not the demands of work as much as the way the demands were made that irritated her. Her employer knew how much time the employees spent on the telephone and whether these calls were business or personal. He checked how often they visited the washroom. It humiliated Dolores to be monitored.

She got up and went to the telephone. She dialed quickly, afraid that if she hesitated she would not complete the call. She listened to the ringing at the other end and began to drum her long nails on the counter top. After five rings she was ready to hang up and was removing the receiver from her ear just as a voice answered sleepily. Dolores smiled and said, "Hello, Jeff. How are you?" She spoke as if it were a normal time to be calling, did not apologise for the lateness of the call. Good strategy, she thought. Pretend all is well and throw him off guard.

"Dolores?" Jeff sounded doubtful. "Yes," she said brightly. "It's me. Surprised?" Before he could answer, she continued cheerily. "So how are you doing? What's become of you these days?"

"Well, for one thing, I got married," Jeff said bluntly. He sounded very annoyed and no wonder: it was now a quarter to three in the middle of the week. But Jeff was more puzzled than annoyed. The call was very unlike the self-sufficient, ordered, business-like Dolores he remembered.

"Is everything all right?" he asked. His tone was solicitous and Dolores noted it. She wanted to be pitied but answered him brightly, "Oh yes. I was up and suddenly thought about you, so I decided to phone you. But so sorry I disturbed you. Do apologise to your wife for me. I'll have to meet her one day."

She rang off and replaced the receiver on the hook thoughtfully. "So the old so-and-so got married without telling me," she said to the shiny white counter top. She sat at the counter for awhile, thinking about where her life was going. Then she felt again that someone was watching her. No skylight this time. She very slowly looked out each kitchen window. Then she saw him. At first just his eyes, then as her eyes grew accustomed to looking out into the dark she made out his face and the colour of his shirt. Very slowly she looked away, her mind racing as he stared at her as she sat. She knew he was the man who had watched her from the skylight. She recognised him in a general sort of way—had remembered the blend of colours in his shirt and had described it to the police.

She got up casually and went up the stairs to call the police. Before long a car turned into the driveway and she heard noise and scuffling. She went downstairs and waited to hear the police knock and call out to her. When she let them in she realised her knees were shaking. She got herself a shot of brandy. As she held the brandy snifter she watched her hands shake.

It turned out she had hired the man to paint her house last summer. He remembered that her house had a skylight and decided to snoop. He claimed no interest in entering the house but confessed he got a kick out of lying on her roof and watching her sleep. He claimed he watched her for four nights. Dolores had not noticed him until the fourth night. This was the first time he had watched her in the kitchen. The police felt he would have eventually tried to gain entry to her house. After the police left, Dolores tried to relax but could not. The prowler was locked up so she was not worried about him returning, but she still felt nervous. Her house no longer felt safe; she had lost her centre.

The next morning Dolores woke with a headache. She walked into her office wearing her sunglasses and kept them on after she took off her coat and got settled. Her employer arrived at her desk within minutes after she sat down. He always came to her office first thing in the morning, no matter how early Dolores got there to try to avoid him. He seemed unable to start his day without chatting to her first. He thought it flattering, but Dolores found it very annoying because she considered it a covert pass but could not put him in his place as she would have liked. At times her employer's morning forays into her office left her so angry, so resentful, that she worried she would explode and tell him off.

"And he is married, too, the little coward," Dolores said to her friend Marianne at lunch that day. "He's married, but he still manages to come into my office every morning and do his little number that makes him feel like cock of the roost for the rest of the day."

Marianne also worked for him, but as she always told Dolores, "Fortunately, he never notices me. He likes Black women."

"Gee thanks," Dolores said. The two women laughed, then Dolores continued, "Marianne, you have no idea how annoying it is. He hears me come in and gives me two minutes to take off my coat and then he's in my office, bringing me a cup of coffee and smiling."

He would compliment her on what she was wearing, then sit smiling at her while they both sipped their coffee, searching for small talk to keep him in her office. Next he would get up and remark that they had to get down to business and begin to nag Dolores about what she was working on. He returned periodically throughout the day, in the belief that his visits kept her at her work. Some days he spent so much time checking on her and her four co-workers' work that they were left with very little time in which to do it. One day Dolores clocked him into her office at ten o'clock and out at half past; he had spent thirty minutes telling her what he wanted her to do over the next week. His instructions had been the same the day before and would not change the day after.

Her attempts to explain to him that he wasted valuable time telling her things he had already told her met with rants that she lacked understanding of his responsibility for the work. At least twice she felt compelled to apologise for the way she had spoken to him; eventually she had expressed her regret that he had been so upset. It was not as much as he had demanded, but she assumed he had decided to compromise.

Dolores began to scan the career sections of the newspapers and put the word out tentatively to contacts she felt she could trust in the industry. The firm wrote speeches for executives and essays for university students and ran a typing service. Dolores wrote history, political science and sociology essays and supervised the typists. At election time she wrote speeches for would-be politicians from the Caribbean who were trying their hand at the political scene, most for the first time, and who couldn't afford the big public relations firms.

Some had won seats and she was quite proud of that. She told herself, "Girl, you should run yourself! You have more brains than they do! And you would have read the speeches better than they did too!"

Although Dolores found her employer tiresome that morning it felt normal to hear him go on. She did not know how she was going to face her house that night, and as his words flew past, she felt safer because of familiarity with his tirade. At least he just talks, she thought, smiling at him. He was in the middle of a particularly nasty, nagging piece of his diatribe and her smile threw him off-guard.

"What?" he said. "Is my fly open?" He gave Dolores a sly grin. She looked at his fly and said, "No, your fly isn't open. Why?"

He looked embarrassed. He could not think of a quick comeback, so he said casually, "Why are you smiling then?"

"Nothing," she replied, no longer smiling. Her look said: drop it or risk looking really silly. Dolores imagined she could hear him weighing the choice. He really is a most irritating, transparent man, she thought. By now he had quite lost his point and Dolores did not help him. She simply sat and waited. Eventually, he petered out and left her office.

By the end of the day Dolores was so exhausted that she wondered how she would drive home. Her whole body ached and she felt sure her teeth and hair hurt, although the possibility of that happening seemed remote. She closed her briefcase and picked up her car keys. What next, she wondered? She had phoned her lover to tell him about the prowler, had waited for him to offer to come and see her that evening. When no offer came she had asked him if he could visit her that evening as she felt a bit nervous.

She felt rather than heard the hesitation in his voice when he said, "Perhaps. I'll give you a call." She had probed, "Are you going to be busy at home?" "No, no," he said, "I'm just a bit tired and had planned to get an early night."

When he rang off she had the distinct feeling that he had done so impatiently, although there was nothing he had said that would confirm it. She felt distinctly unwanted and unloved.

She eased her steel-grey European car into the rush hour traffic on the highway. She sighed; usually, there were things that cheered her up, but she did not even feel up to going anywhere. She was too tired to stay awake through a movie; she did not feel like going out to dinner alone; and anyway, the idea of being out was not at all appealing. What she really needed was a nice warm bath and a nap.

She had inserted a CD into the player without checking to see what it was. The music she kept in the car was all carefully selected to soothe frazzled nerves. She always felt tense driving home in the rush hour traffic and eased her car into the fast lane. She did not like to drive yet enjoyed the rush of power that came with pushing a good car at top speed. She had the traffic tickets that went with speeding but felt they were worth it.

She turned up the volume to hear Al Jarreau and Randy Crawford belt out: *Suddenly you struck me just like lightning!* She sang along with them feeling free, speeding along the highway ... free and fast. Free like she felt when she went home to St. Kitts. There she could be herself and could talk like she felt like talking and dance like she felt like dancing and eat the way she felt like eating. She relaxed into those Kittician-girl feelings and began to let go of the day's frustrations and last night's terror.

By the time Dolores turned into her driveway she felt like a sack of potatoes: dirty and bumpy and heavy. Annoyed at the house for failing to provide the security she had so carefully planned for, she turned her key in the front door lock in a very different mood than yesterday's. "What's the use?" she asked aloud. "What's the use of going to the trouble of creating a beautiful home only to have somebody just come along and spoil it? What's the use of being beautiful and successful when there is nobody to share it with? My friends are busy with their own families. They don't have time for me. What's the use?"

She had done all of the right things, but they had not paid off. She had gone after and got the right training, the right job, the right house, the right clothes, the right car. She had gone after the right man, too, only to meet him when it was too late. She had bought the right home only to have an intruder destroy her feelings of peace.

She went into the living room and sat on the couch for a long time without turning on the lights before getting up to go upstairs to her bedroom, where she changed into black silk lounging pajamas. She went into the bathroom and took out a bottle of pills from the medicine cabinet. Then she went downstairs to the kitchen to get a crystal goblet from the china cabinet in the dining room. After filling it with mineral water from the refrigerator she went back to the dark living room. She sat in a large antique chair with a soft, padded seat for several hours, the glass of water in one hand and the pills in the other.

The telephone did not ring once nor did the doorbell. She got up and put on a CD, returned to her chair and picked up the bottle of pills. She emptied the half-full bottle into her hand and sighed. As she threw the pills into the back of her mouth she reached for the crystal goblet on the coffee table.

She swallowed the pills as Joan Armatrading's voice bellowed from the speakers: *Father, I have tried and tried, Mother I have tried and tried, I did it your way. Now I do it my way.* The telephone rang later. But Jeff hung up after several rings, having decided he would drop by Dolores's house the next day to see if she was all right. Soaring above her body, Dolores's spirit appreciated his concern.

How You Panty Get Wet?

How you panty get wet? How you panty get wet? No rain was falling. Sun was shining. How you panty get wet? The two girls skipped down the street, their voices vibrant and clear, enjoying the new song they had learned in the schoolyard that day. They reached their gate, unlatched it and went into the yard, still singing, when Cyntie heard the beating coming.

Her mother's hurrying steps were the warning. Then Cyntie heard the leather strap hitting her mother's palm. By then it was too late to do anything to save herself and Violet. Cyntie looked up as her mother's arm descended. Still engrossed in singing the new song at top voice, Violet did not see the beating coming. Her high-pitched treble rang out: *No rain was falling. Sun was shining....*

She never finished the line. The strap came down *whoosh*. Violet screamed as the thick leather connected with the flesh beneath the thin cotton fabric of her school uniform. They got four licks each, their mother holding each by the wrist with her left hand while she wielded the strap with her right. She was a strong woman. They were wiry and thin. The licks were punctuated by her irate voice. "I don't send you school to learn how you panty get wet. Learn sense, not nonsense!"

Afterwards the children bawled loudly. Their mother shouted at them. "Stop de noise! You get anyting to cry for?"

They nursed their bruises silently, hiccupping jerkily as they sniffled and wiped ineffectively at the tears running down their faces. Cyntie decided then and there that she truly hated her mother.

Miss John, Cyntie's Sunday School teacher, gave them a verse to learn: "Honour thy father and thy mother that thy days may be long in the land which the Lord thy God giveth thee." Wanting to please Miss John, Cyntie learned the verse by heart. She liked her very much. She was one of the few big people who treated Cyntie like a human being. All the other big people, including her mother and father and her uncle, treated children as if they were stupid. Miss John was different. She always smiled at the children and asked "How youall today?" Then she listened for their answer, prompting them when they did not reply. "Nobody answering me? How youall? I hope allyou well?"

Some other big people would sometimes ask the same question, but they would not wait for the answer. They would begin talking to each other right away while Cyntie was trying to think of how she was. She knew that she could have quickly answered, "Well, tank you." That is what people said when asked how they were, but she wanted to answer something different. For instance, she would sometimes answer Miss John, "Not too bad today, Miss John." Other times she would say, "Fine!" trying to imitate Miss Pinkton, the Peace Corps lady who lived on her street.

Miss Pinkton said "fine" with a roll, stretching out each letter with her American accent. To Cyntie's Antiguan ears, it sounded like "f-ah-hn!" She liked to hear Miss Pinkton say it and she liked to hear herself say it too. Most of the time she said it softly to herself when she was sitting alone on the steps of the house. Sometimes while her teacher was talking, Cyntie would remember Miss Pinkton's "f-ah-hn!" and would suddenly mutter it under her breath.

Cyntie was very proud of herself when Miss John called on her to recite the line about thy father and thy mother. She stood up straight and said the verse clearly and without hesitation. Miss John said, "That was beautiful, Cynthia, thank you." Then she smiled straight through to Cyntie's heart.

But Miss John was not finished. She asked her, "Cynthia, do you honour your father and your mother?"

Cyntie was startled. For one thing she did not know what "honour" meant and had not thought to ask anyone to explain it. She had an idea that the verse had something to do with obeying her father and her mother. She did not want to make a mistake, so she told Miss John that she did not know what it meant to honour thy father and thy mother.

Cyntie listened quietly while Miss John explained. "The way you talk to your mother and father and what you think in your mind will tell if you honour them or not," Miss John said. "Remember: thought, word and deed are important. Not just word and deed. So you should honour your father and mother in your thoughts too."

That evening in the bath, Violet reminded Cyntie, "Miss John want us to love Mammy Ellen an Papa and be polite and mannersable to them so we have to behave better from now on."

Cyntie said "choopse" and blew her nose loudly. Life was very straightforward to her. She was still nursing a sore back from the beating.

"Even when we get licks?" she asked. Violet looked at her sister and laughed. Cyntie's face looked so funny when she pushed out her mouth and her chin. "You look like Brutus when he barking at somebody passing down de street," she said. Eventually Cyntie laughed too.

The day Cyntie and Violet got licks for singing "How You Panty Get Wet?" their mother went into town to buy some fabric. That evening, just before the two girls went to bed, they noticed their mother cutting out the fabric. Violet to Mammy Ellen, leaned on her knee and asked, "What you making, Mammy Ellen?" She just too fast to go sleep until she know what Mammy Ellen cutting out, Cyntie thought sullenly. Violet had no shame. The least she could have done was to be silent for the night just to teach their mother a lesson. Their mother looked happy that Violet had asked her about the cloth. She want to show off to somebody, Cyntie thought.

Their father had come home late from work and had fallen asleep as soon as he finished his tea. It was only because Papa sleeping why she showing Violet she cloth, thought Cyntie.

Mammy Ellen stroked Violet's chin. "You like it, chile?" Violet nodded. Then their mother had looked over at Cyntie who stood nearby, feigning a lack of interest. "You like it, too, Cyntie?" Mammy Ellen asked. Cyntie nodded. Still refusing to speak, she had smoothed a corner of the plastic tablecloth on their dining table, pretending to be absorbed in de-creasing the folds in the plastic. Then she took a matchstick and began to scrape out the dirt lodged in the tablecloth. She diligently scraped the curled leaf of each rosebud, exhaling exaggeratedly to blow the dirt off the end of the matchstick. Mammy Ellen held up the cloth against her bosom and smiled at her daughters. "I making a nice dress for Carnival."

Violet smiled back at her, "Is nice, Mammy Ellen. You go look good in it."

Their mother laughed. "You tink so, eh Violet? Well dat good cause dis is what I going wear next week." Mammy Ellen always made herself a new dress for Carnival Monday, when she took Cyntie and Violet into town and let them stand at the corner near the fence by Barclays Bank to watch the goings-on in the street.

Cyntie had heard her mother telling her aunt that their father was working hard to save money to buy a piece of land in Villa. It used to be that they would always have new dresses for Easter, Harvest and Christmas. Now Cyntie could not remember when last she had had a new dress. When she had outgrown her shoes she had not wanted to say anything to her mother and had told her instead that she wanted the toes cut out of her shoes to make them look pretty. Her mother had refused until one day she caught Cyntie limping home from Sunday School. "Cyntie!" she called out from the front window as Cyntie and Violet reached the house. "You shoes too tight?" her mother had asked in a voice full of accusation.

Cyntie had not tried to lie. She knew her mother well enough to know when it was time to give in. "Yes," she had admitted, hanging her head.

"Why you didn't tell me?" Mammy Ellen had cupped her oldest daughter's chin and raised her face up to see her eyes. Cyntie had cast her eyes downward.

"You don't want a new shoes? You like dis one and want to keep it?" Cyntie had nodded. The next day her mother came to meet Cyntie after school and had taken her into town and bought her a new pair of shoes.

Cyntie knelt beside the bed next to Violet to say her prayers. She thought about how her mother was buying herself a new dress for Carnival and about how she, Cyntie, had been ready to do without a new pair of shoes. She remembered how her shoes used to hurt her feet so badly that she sometimes used to feel tears of pain near her eyes. Sure that she was not honouring her mother, as she said her prayers, she silently asked for forgiveness for having such bad thoughts. But even as she tried to pray for forgiveness, she found she was still angry.

When Carnival Monday came, Mammy Ellen cooked the food for the day early so as not to have to worry about it while she was in town. Her husband would come into town later and meet her in case she needed help with the children on the way home. He had a group of friends he played dominoes with on his days off and would play with them until later in the afternoon. He was a quiet man who did not like the big crowds and went into town at Carnival time only to make sure they were safe.

Confident that all was settled, Mammy Ellen sent the children to bathe. Then she gave herself a sponge bath in her bedroom, using just a little water in the bathpan she kept under her bed. She was careful to mix her bathwater with some hot water she had heated on the coal pot. No matter what time it was, she made sure that her bathwater was warm. It would not do to give herself a chill. As she dried her skin with the little towel she kept in the bedroom, she called out, "Cyntie! Violet!"

They answered in unison. "Yes, Mammy Ellen?"

Their mother paused to make sure she had their attention. "Finish you bath an come an put on you clothes. Is time we go in town for de jump-up."

On the bed in their bedroom lay two dresses, sized for Cyntie and Violet, made from the fabric Mammy Ellen had bought for her Carnival dress. The girls turned to look at their mother. She stood behind them, smiling. Violet spoke first. "But you tell us it was you dress!"

"Yes, ah wanted to fool you. Ent you surprised?" Violet nodded and said yes, but Cyntie could not speak.

Appearing not to notice Cyntie's silence, Mammy Ellen shooed at them to get them moving, "Good," she said. "Dat's good. Now get dress. Hurry, else we going miss de first float."

It was only after they were fully dressed and out of the house that Cyntie realised Mammy Ellen was wearing one of her old Sunday dresses. Catching her mother's eye, she startled herself by saying, "Ah love you, Mammy Ellen."

Her mother looked at her in pleased surprise; they never told each other things like that. Then copying her sister, Violet said, "Ah love you, too, Mammy Ellen. Tanks for de dress an ah sorry you don't have a new dress too."

Cyntie swallowed noisily and said to her mother, "Ah honour you, Mammy Ellen." She felt tears on her cheeks. Mammy Ellen hugged her two daughters close and wiped Cyntie's tears. "I honour you, too, chile." She passed the back of her right hand across her eyes. Then she stood up straight and took their hands. "Come leh we go in town."

Mammy Ellen stood at the Barclays Bank corner, tightly holding her daughters' hands. The bands were big this year, too big for Mammy Ellen and her daughters, so they stood on the corner, waiting for a band to pass by that was not too rowdy. Mammy Ellen wanted to make sure that they could jump up safely. At her age she could not properly protect two small children in a large crowd. Finally Harmonites steelband came across Market Street on the way home to The Point. Mammy Ellen said to Cyntie and Violet, "Maybe we will take dis one cause we know dem and dey going our way. Besides, de crowd not too bad."

As they jumped up beside the band Cyntie began to make out the song and turned fearfully to look at her mother. Mammy Ellen was singing, smiling first at Violet on her left then at Cyntie on her right. Cyntie joined in, as Violet, too, began to sing: *How you panty get wet? How you panty get wet? No rain was falling. Sun was shining. How you panty get wet?*

Sister Friends
Is Sister Friends

Beatrice heaved herself out of her chair to open the door for Irene. She knew it was Irene knocking on the front door because Irene came to see her the same time every evening, except Fridays. Irene never came on Fridays. She was an Adventist and Adventists were not allowed to walk about after their sabbath began at six o'clock on Friday.

The two women were from the same street in The Point and had gone to Point School and to The Antigua Girls' High School together. Friends since they were little girls, when Beatrice and Irene grew up they remained best friends, though their lives were very different.

Beatrice had begun to put on weight in her early teens, but even now, at thirty, Irene was as skinny as a model. When she was twenty-two years old, Beatrice went on a trip to St. Lucia to see her uncle and had come back to Antigua starry-eyed and in love. Within six months a man she met on her trip came to Antigua and married Beatrice, and they produced four children in eight years. Beatrice put on more weight, while Irene remained slim, unmarried and childless.

As Beatrice moved heavily across the room to open the door for Irene, she called out to her husband who was resting in bed, "Devon! Irene come! Go take the children for dey walk, nuh?"

Devonshire was a most congenial man. He was also a very handsome man; so much so that when he had first come to Antigua, people were surprised that Beatrice had managed to get him. They would look from his Harry Belafonte handsomeness to Beatrice's African features and her weight and wonder behind her back what he saw in her. Beatrice herself did not understand what Devonshire saw in her. She thought herself big and fat, and though she did not think she was ugly, she did not consider herself beautiful, even though Devonshire told her that she was.

Beatrice *was* beautiful. She had round clear eyes framed by long eyelashes; but her mouth was her most beautiful feature. It was wide, and her lips were two thick petals that parted to reveal even, white teeth when she smiled. Her cheeks dimpled and so did her chin. Devonshire liked to tell her jokes, just to make her laugh and open up the flower that was her mouth. Her smile would light up her face, and Devonshire would laugh with her and say, "I could watch you laugh all day. You look so pretty wid you dimples, Bee."

As Irene came into the house Devonshire got up and called to the children, who were playing in the yard. He had promised Beatrice that he would get them out of the way so she and Irene could have some privacy. He always tried to cooperate by keeping the four youngsters occupied when Irene came to visit. They were still young and boisterous and Devonshire liked giving Beatrice a break. He was used to his wife's getting together with Irene every week. It had been that way ever since he came to Antigua eight years ago, and he saw no rea son to stand in the way of their friendship.

The two women sat down. Irene was alarmed at what Beatrice had told her that morning. She had come to her workplace in the bank to say, "Irene, I want to talk to you. Is very serious. You coming for sure tonight?" Irene had nodded nervously.

"It's about Devon," Beatrice had said, and then seeing Irene's supervisor frown at them, she had hurriedly left the bank. Irene had spent the rest of the day seeing Beatrice's usually happy face twisted into a frown. She knew her friend was not a worrier, so it must mean there was something to worry about. She sat on the edge of a chair and waited for Beatrice to speak.

As for Beatrice, she was so relaxed that she did not notice that her friend was nervous. She was a little worried, but she felt in control of the situation. "Girl," she said, "is a little trouble I heard, and I was really worried when I come by your workplace this morning, but now it's not so bad."

She paused as Devonshire brought the children in from the yard to say good afternoon to Irene. As soon as the door closed behind them, Beatrice continued, "I don't know nothing 'bout men, Irene, you know dat. Devon is de first man I know and I never be wid any other man, so is real trouble for me to know how to take tings. But let me tell you how it go."

She leaned towards her friend as she spoke and touched her on the arm. Irene jumped at her touch, and for the first time it registered with Beatrice that Irene was nervous. She looked at her gratefully, pleased that Irene cared enough to be nervous for her. "I know you does work in town so you more worldly-wise and could tell me how to take dis. Is Devon on me mind, as I tell you dis morning."

Irene looked even more alarmed. "What happen to Devon? What you mean?"

Beatrice hurried on. "Somebody tell me dis morning dat how Devon have a next woman he does go visit every Friday night. Dey say is years now he doing it and, girl, I sit down and I tink 'bout it. Ever since 'bout de second week dat Devon come Antigua he been busy every Friday night. Come hell or high water, dat man leave dis house every single Friday night for eight years. But he does tell me he going out wid his friend and I never doubt him. You know his friend from St. Lucia who married that girl from Seatons?"

She hardly paused for Irene's nod. "And besides," Beatrice went on, "dat friend does pick him up religiously every Friday night and does bring him back home too. I does see him with me own two eye."

Irene felt a ringing in her ears and it seemed like Beatrice receded to another place and time. "He does come home real late every Friday night, but girl, if you man can't take a little night out wid friends what kind a life is dat? What you tink?"

Irene shrugged her shoulders but did not look at Beatrice. Beatrice wondered if Irene had also heard the story about Devon and some other woman and had not known how to tell her all these years.

"Eight years de woman said. Irene, you tink is true? You don't hear nothing like dat?"

By now Irene knew how she must answer. "No, I don't hear nothing like dat." Then she said a little angrily, "Why people does talk so much? Is who tell you so anyway, Bee?"

"Well, I promise not to tell nobody is who tell me, but I can tell you. You and me is sister friends." She lowered her voice and continued, "Girl, is Miss Peters meet me by Bryson dis morning and stop me in de street and tell me so. She say she know who de woman be, too, but she say she not telling me is who. You know, me shouldn't listen to she because her husband leave her and living with a young, young woman in a house in Potters. She just want to see everybody else unhappy—ever since dat man leave and go she been a miserable person."

She looked at Irene for confirmation and Irene nodded. She did not trust herself to speak.

Devonshire returned from his walk with the children to find Beatrice and Irene sitting outside on the step talking quietly together. He greeted them jovially and took the children inside the house to give them their supper. He had no idea that he had been the topic of conversation.

Irene got up to leave. "Well, Bee, I will see you Saturday night after evening service as usual. You know I don't walk 'bout on Fridays so you not seeing me tomorrow."

Beatrice patted her on the arm. "Girl, is good I have you for a friend. I really glad I could talk to somebody about dat stupidness because I was really upset dis morning, you know? I feel stupid dat I waste time talking about it, in truth." Irene smiled, then, calling out her goodbyes to the children and to Devonshire, she left. Beatrice watched her go down the steps and sighed as she admired her friend's slim figure moving gracefully down the street. She went into the house to help Devonshire with the children, aware each movement was heavy and clumsy from the excess weight she carried on her small frame.

Around seven o'clock the next evening, as Beatrice and the children were finishing supper, Devonshire prepared to leave with his friend. With his usual affection he kissed Beatrice on the cheek and said, "You looking sad. You all right?" Beatrice nodded and smiled.

He said, "I going buy some ice cream to cheer you up when I coming home later, okay?"

Beatrice searched his face for guilt. "Where you going find ice cream dem hour you does come home?" She looked closely at him but saw nothing unusual in his reaction.

Devonshire noticed her unusual curtness. Hugging her close to him, he said, "Baby, I going find ice cream for you. If I see it getting late and dem fellahs still liming, I will make Winston take me to buy de ice cream for you and den go back."

Beatrice thought: "If he could call on Winston to drive home, he could not be with any woman." She was ashamed of herself for doubting him. After Devonshire left, Beatrice hummed a little tune as she tidied up the house, thinking about her talk with Irene the night before and feeling glad she had managed to put the foolishness about Devonshire and another woman aside. Other women she knew had husbands who paid no attention to them in the house—never mind noticing when they were not feeling quite up to scratch.

"I lucky bad," she thought, "I have a man who always tinking 'bout how I feel, and look at dat, I nearly doubt him. He would be so vex if he knew I was listening to gossip about him. He tell me long time ago dat plenty people want us to mash up and he right. People jealous of me and going tell me bad tings 'bout him cause he bang water come here."

Beatrice thought of Irene and how lucky she was to have

such a good friend. "Is not my sabbath," she thought, "so I could walk about. I must go and visit Irene. The problem is de children. I can't leave dem by deyself."

She went out to her backyard and called to her neighbour, who also had small children, to ask her to keep an eye on the children. The neighbour agreed and Beatrice set out at eight o'clock to visit Irene. Walking slowly because her weight made it hard for her to get any speed without puffing and panting, she enjoyed the cool night. The ladies of the night were in full bloom in her aunt's front yard, and they sweetened the air. Her aunt was sitting on her gallery, and Beatrice stopped to ask her for a piece of the shrub to carry for Irene. Setting off again, she sniffed the branch on the way, looking forward to seeing Irene smile and thank her for the little gift of flowers. They were always doing nice things like that for each other.

As she turned the corner to Irene's street she began to get a bad feeling in the bottom of her belly. She slowed down her steps, coming to a standstill outside Irene's house. She stood there for a full minute, then shook herself and opened the gate. The ladies of the night smelled sickly sweet as she walked up to the house.

"The last time I feel like dis is when Papa dead and I bend down to put dese same flowers on his grave," she thought as she heaved herself up the three steps to her friend's house. She knocked on the door, wondering if anything was wrong with Irene but not wanting even to think of that possibility.

After she knocked, Beatrice heard low, muffled voices from inside the house. Irene had company. Beatrice called out, "Irene is me, Bee." There was a scuffling sound and more muf-

fled talk. Beatrice suddenly realised she had probably inter-
rupted Irene with a man. She considered leaving, but then
Irene called out to her, "I coming. I was sleeping."

Beatrice waited for Irene to come to the door. By now she
had a broad smile on her face, pleased she had caught Irene
with a man. Irene opened the door and let her friend into the
house. She was wearing a loose house dress and her hair was
dishevelled. Smoothing down her hair, she said, "Girl, I was
tired so I just come home and go straight to me bed. I didn't
even eat nothing. You know my sabbath prevent me from
cooking after sundown."

Irene spoke very nervously and did not look at Beatrice.
Beatrice laughed. "Irene is me you talking to, you know. If you
see youself. Sure I know you not suppose to cook on you sabbath. You forget I does send food give you every Friday afternoon with Miss Kate? Why you tink I does send it? Cause I
love to cook? Is to help you out with you sabbath."

Beatrice lowered her voice. With a giggle she whispered, "I
hear you in dere talking to a man. Is who? How you never tell
me you have man? And we is sister friend. You couldn't come by
me, but you could be with man on you sabbath, and you could-
n't cook, but you could be with man. Girl, you sly bad."

Just then Beatrice caught sight of a pair of shoes tucked
under a chair at Irene's little table. She looked from the shoes
to Irene. Irene followed Beatrice's glance and froze. Woodenly
Beatrice walked into Irene's bedroom, looked at Devonshire,
then turned back out to the living room. Balling her hand into
a fist, she punched Irene in the mouth. Coming alive with the
blow, she spat in Irene's face. "Dat's for all dem Friday night
you didn't come by me. Talk 'bout you sabbath begin."

She hit Irene again, this time catching her in the belly. "Dat's for spending de time wid my husband while you eating me food. You is some sister friend."

She turned and picked up Devonshire's shoes, calling out to him: "Devon, come boy. Put you clothes on. Don't frighten, we going home. Come."

Butterskin Going Catch You

From the time Lesroy met Philomena it was wine and roses all the way. She was so good-looking, had such pretty brown skin—"butterskin" his friend Sello called it. Sello himself was not partial to butterskin women, but he recognised that Lesroy had that weakness and he used to tease him about it. "Eh, Lesroy, man. I see you out wid a woman wid de sweetest butterskin. Where you find all dese women wid de same skin?" and Sello would laugh and hold his head back. Lesroy would just suck his teeth and not answer. He was used to being teased by Sello about the sameness of his women: brown-skinned, the colour of golden butter.

With Philomena, though, Lesroy knew right away that she was different. She unlocked a part of him that had been untouched. He would see her walking towards him on the street and his heart would beat faster and louder. Then when she came up to him he would be all shy and tongue-tied—something very unusual for Lesroy, who had always had the upper hand with women. Usually they loved him and he accepted their love and gave back bits of himself when it suited him. But with Philomena he became all lovey-lovey, like when he was a little boy and his mother would hug him.

It took Lesroy a long time to court Philomena. For one thing she said she could not go out with him because he did not have a car. When she was in Trinidad she had grown used to being driven in cars, and she was not prepared to settle for less just because she was in Antigua. Lesroy promised her he was buying a car and that he would ask her out again once he had one.

As soon as he told Sello about it he regretted it. Sello had laughed till he held his belly. "Where you going get motor car? Boy, what happen to you? You make a little woman have you as if you head cook. So what you going do now?"

"Buy a car," Lesroy said evenly. And he meant it. Whatever it would take to get Philomena, he meant to do. He spent the better part of each day thinking about her. One day as he was building Mr. James's house he saw Philomena's face in front of him and forgot that he was hammering a nail. The next thing he knew, he had hit his finger and was yelling in pain. It got bloodshot and ached for weeks afterwards.

Finally Lesroy bought the car. It was so old that it rattled when he drove it over the pot-holes in the streets, but he did not care: it was a car and now Philomena would talk to him and go out with him. No longer would he have to satisfy himself with saying, "Hello Philomena," when she walked past him and Sello as they sat on the little bridge on the corner. Once in awhile he even managed to walk a few steps beside her, but she always ended up chasing him away, saying, "Listen, I can't be seen wid any man. Me aunt would be vex wid me."

Lesroy would turn back dejectedly and console himself that he had managed to step beside her, had smelled her perfume and got a close look at her beautiful face. He liked the way her top lip curled with little hairs above it. Very sexy, he thought. She had long hair under her arms, too, and Lesroy could even smell her perspiration mixed with her deodorant as she swung her handbag. She always wore sleeveless dresses, so he would sneak a look at the long, silky hair on her underarms and feel his manhood rise. Afterwards, he would daydream of rubbing his nose and his lips in her armpits.

But what Lesroy loved about Philomena most was her nice butterskin colour. He also liked her hips, especially the way she swung them when she walked. She danced when she walked and when he watched her, he always found himself thinking about the way Sparrow and Nelson danced on stage. Philomena had a nice bottom, too—not too big and not too small. Just right. It used to make him have to turn away from Sello until he had cooled himself down.

The car was going to change everything. He could not wait to see Philomena's face. He was sure she liked him and was just waiting for him to buy the car. He stood at the corner with Sello, looking over the car parked right on the corner, waiting to take Philomena home or for a drive. She came walking down the street, pretending as usual not to see them, so Lesroy had to fight to get her attention. He did not mind her playing hard to get.

This time he approached her with a little more confidence than usual. Because he had the car he felt more like a man with something going for him. "Would you want a drive home?" he asked formally and with a bit of stiffness in his voice. Philomena looked at him in disbelief. "You have a car?"

"Yes, look it over dere," said Lesroy, lapsing into his normal speech. "I buy it today. So now you can go out wid me den."

Sello watched as Philomena stepped over to Lesroy's car and got in. He had never really expected her to notice Lesroy and was still not convinced that it was really happening. As they drove off, Lesroy turned and waved to Sello. "See you later!" Sello barely managed to nod.

Within a few days Lesroy had Philomena in the back seat of the car. He wondered for a brief moment if she would have got close with him if he had never bought a car, but he was so happy with this woman who smelled so sweet and fresh that he dismissed the thought. The only other time he smelled anything so sweet and fresh was Anjos store with the big statue of a dog in the window.

The next thing Lesroy knew, he was taking Philomena home after a little drive in the country one day when she told him that she thought she was pregnant. Lesroy was not particularly concerned: he had three children with three women already and did not mind having another baby. Besides, this was one way to bind Philomena to him. He did not have any sons yet, and he hoped that maybe she would bear him one.

"I hope you will have a boy," he said and kissed her on the cheek. Philomena was crying. "What happen?" he asked her. "You tink I would say is not mine?" She shook her head. "Den why you crying so hard? You don't want to have our baby?"

Philomena cried harder and Lesroy was obliged to hold her until she stopped. He felt very insecure about her again, having decided she was crying because she did not want to have his baby. But Philomena explained that her aunt would be very angry with her. Philomena had come to Antigua to do better and now she was going to have a baby without being married.

Lesroy had never considered marriage. He had always known that he would get married some day, but that was something he would do in the very distant future, when he was much older and much more settled financially. He told Philomena this and she burst into tears again.

"Now you take me best favours and you want me to have a illegitimate child. You too wicked Lesroy, you too wicked."

Lesroy heard himself saying, "Well, maybe we should get married den, what you tink?"

Philomena turned a dazzling smile on him and Lesroy knew he did not stand a chance. He was so in love with Philomena that he did not mind getting married, really. It was just too sudden, and besides, he lived with his old grandmother, and she had only a little two-room house. He had always planned to build his own house before he got married. He told his grandmother about Philomena and the baby coming.

"Is all right," said his grandmother. "Bring her to live wid us. I will manage. But only ting, Lesroy. You sure you know dis woman? Trinidad woman is bad woman, you know. What you know 'bout her?"

Lesroy had to admit that he did not know anything much about Philomena. She had never told him about her life in Trinidad except to say that her father lived there and would kill Lesroy if he didn't marry her. Lesroy had heard about Trinidadian men and how violent they were. When he was a little boy a man named Boysie Singh and another Singh, a doctor, had killed a whole set of people. Boysie Singh killed the people by pretending to carry them over to Venezuela, and the other Singh doctor killed his wife and some other people. Lesroy thought this to be true, but he wasn't sure.

He remembered, too, that a man named Malik had killed another whole set of people in Trinidad and even a woman from England and his own friends and buried them right in his own backyard. So Lesroy decided that he loved Philomena anyway. And besides, he did not want any violence from her father in his life.

The day of the wedding came, and Lesroy found himself in church looking very sharp. His best man was Sello, and Philomena's father had come up from Trinidad to be her father-giver. Just as Lesroy had suspected, Philomena's father looked very fierce and kept on asking Lesroy questions: how much money he made, how much he paid for the car, when he planned to build a house and how many children he planned to give Philomena. Lesroy could answer only some of the questions because the truth was, he had not made any plans about house and children at all. But he was so afraid of Philomena's father that he made up answers, hoping that they were the right ones. Some were not. Lesroy noticed that when he said, for instance, that he planned to give Philomena two children, her father looked very upset and asked him point-blank, "Why? You don't like children?"

Lesroy hastily said, "Oh yes, I love children, but I just want to take it easy at first. Maybe we will have some more later," he added, at a loss as to what would constitute a sufficient number.

Then Philomena's father asked Lesroy if he planned to buy his own house or rent for awhile. Again trying to please the man Lesroy said, "I plan to buy my own house, sir." Philomena's father looked at him with real suspicion this time, "Wid what money? You going win pools?"

Lesroy sighed and said, "No, but I will save up." At that Philomena's father laughed and said, "Oh ho! You plan to save up. Boy, you will be saving forever if dat is de money you making. Listen, I go buy a house for you and Philomena before I go back to Trinidad. Yes, de way you talking, my daughter going be catching she royal in you grandmother house for a long time."

The wedding went off without too many hitches, except for Sello forgetting where he had put the ring. As Lesroy sweated in his rented clothes, Sello patted his old-time suit, borrowed from his father, then searched each pocket until at last he produced the ring from his back fob pocket. By the time Sello finally pulled out the ring the minister was looking up to heaven for support. He had had enough of this wedding party. Philomena had arrived at the church a whole hour late and had started stepping down the aisle in the wedding slow-step with her four bridesmaids, three flower girls and a page boy all going one-two, one-two, behind her.

The minister had shooed them along quite shamelessly, even though he was standing at the altar. He did not care. This was his last wedding before his transfer back to England. He sometimes doubted that he had sprung from Antiguan roots and spoke all the time about his parish just outside of London. He had a house there, too, so he now felt that his roots were definitely somewhere else. He frowned at the bride and her slow-stepping troops and made a sound of annoyance as he hustled them up to stand in front of him so he could join the man and woman together in holy matrimony.

Philomena and Lesroy did not seem to notice the minister's annoyance. Even if they had noticed, for quite different reasons they were both too nervous to care. Philomena was excited because at last she was getting married. Lesroy was still in shock at actually finding himself in church, getting married. He loved Philomena; he just had not ever really planned on being married quite so fast.

Just then Sello poked him in the ribs. "Boy, Lesroy. Butterskin, butterskin. Ah tell you butterskin would catch you!"

Lesroy looked at his bride's brown-skinned face and smiled weakly. Then he looked at her father's face and knew he had made the right decision.

Bluebeard in a Concrete Jungle

One morning Junice got up, looked around at her apartment and saw that it looked tired—as tired as she felt of life. She refused to look at her husband, her two sons and her dog. Instead she got dressed and prepared to leave. Her movements did not wake them; even when she walked out the front door, they still slept soundly. Not even the dog stirred as she went quietly down the hall. That was strange: she was used to its bark echoing behind her whenever she left the apartment.

She was alone on the elevator and was relieved that because it was so early there was no one about—no one to whom she had to be polite and cheerful. She thought about when they had first moved into the building and how she had liked the fact that the tenants spoke to each other. It had felt much less impersonal than the other buildings they had lived in. Now it felt like such a chore saying good morning and hello to people all the time.

She walked out to the parking lot; still no one was in sight. It was early, about six o'clock, so not even the building superintendent was up and around. Junice got into the tired old car and drove herself out of the parking lot, feeling as if she were lifting the apartment complex itself off her shoulders as she approached the exit. "Concrete jungle" she said out loud, and the Bob Marley tune came into her head.

She sang the words too. *Concrete jungle! Oh no! Oh no! Oh no! Oh no! Concrete jungle!* and then shook her head sadly. Sometimes it felt as if the jungle were inside her, taking her over, making her all scrunched up as though the buildings had conspired to take her over, making her feel as unwanted as a cockroach.

She turned into the street. It had not occurred to her to decide where to go. She had simply woken up at dawn, feeling miserable, wanting to go somewhere but having nowhere to go. Then she had got up and dressed to go out, but she still had no particular destination in mind. She drove out of her neighbourhood and turned the car in the direction of the highway. That she still did not know where she was going bothered her in a funny kind of way. Are you cracking up, driving without knowing where you're going? she asked herself.

She headed onto the 401 East, and the further she got into Scarborough the more concrete structures she began to see. She sighed, wondering where she would have to drive to escape the spiralling cement. Suddenly the skyscrapers tapered off and she was looking at houses. She still felt she had not escaped the masses of concrete. What was even worse was that the houses all looked alike. She was sure that people sometimes went into the wrong house without noticing. She tried to imagine what it would be like living in one of those houses but could not get any further in her mind than the front garden.

She considered getting off the highway at the first Scarborough exit and going to visit a friend who lived nearby.

Then she thought better of it, not wanting to explain why she was driving around at that hour of the morning. Besides, her friend was married to a most annoying man, and he always leered at Junice, even when his wife was around.

There was no one she wanted to visit and no one she could turn to. Her tears were rolling down her cheeks and dropping onto her collar before Junice realised that she was crying. The tears dripped off her collar and onto her chest until it was wet. She had not cried for years and did not remember crying even when her mother died two years ago. Junice had stood at the graveside, silent even inside, and feeling guilty, too, because she had quarrelled with her mother only two days before she died suddenly from a heart attack.

She did not pull the car over to the side of the highway to dry her face. When she had finished crying she fished tissues out of a box in the glove compartment and blew her nose loudly with one hand while still guiding the car in the flow of the early morning highway traffic with the other. She knew that eventually she would have to stop driving, but she was in no hurry. Not even the thought that her husband would by now have begun to worry about her prompted her to turn back home. She thought of her two sons getting up in the morning and finding their mother gone. For a brief moment she wavered in her resolve to keep on driving. She knew she would have to turn back soon.

Thinking about her husband made her shudder. Their relationship had deteriorated. What really irked Junice was that he seemed to be so happy with the situation, while she could barely tolerate it. He had a spring to his step that she believed was put there by some other woman. He had a smile on his face every day as he got dressed to go to work, as if he could not wait to get himself to his office. Who does he have there? she often wondered. She knew that Stanley did not like his job very much, so she was sure it was some woman that put that smile on his face and that spring in his step.

She did not want to know who the woman was. She had lived through several of Stanley's women and had long moved past the stage where she wanted to identify the woman and accost her. Once, early in their marriage, a woman had been introduced to her as someone Stanley had grown up with and Junice had accepted her as such. Stanley was from Barbados and Junice was from St. Kitts, so she had easily accepted his explanation. Then she began to see things that made her wonder. Every time the woman came to their apartment she looked it up and down and was always very quiet. If it was a party, it was different; then she would pull Stanley up to dance whenever a slow number was playing.

One time she had pressed her body so close to Stanley's that Junice felt her face get hot with anger. Later, after everyone had left, she had asked Stanley about it. He shushed her, telling her that she had a suspicious mind. Jennifer, he scolded, was his childhood friend, like a sister to him.

That was before they were married, when Junice and Stanley used to live together. Then they had their wedding and Jennifer came to the reception dressed to kill in red hot-pants—and that was not what women wore to wedding receptions. Jennifer was the most striking woman there. Everyone else wore African clothes, and Junice had felt drab standing next to Jennifer in those red hot-pants. Who could beat a sexy-looking woman in shorts? Junice had asked herself in the bathroom mirror. Hot-pants my foot, she thought. All they are are glorified shorts, made decent by wearing stockings under them and dressing them up with high heels.

When the number finished Junice saw that the hot-pants were damp in front where Jennifer had pressed herself hard against Stanley. They were made out of red satin, so it did not take much to make them damp. Besides, Jennifer had done quite a lot in them to make them damp, and it had all been against Stanley's crotch.

Junice had avoided looking at Stanley while he danced with Jennifer. Afterwards she had gone outside by herself and sat on the balcony of the church hall. Stanley had come after her and asked her, "You vexed about something?"

Junice had replied, "No, you do something for me to be vexed about?"

It was on that note that they began their marriage.

The night before the wedding, Jennifer had invited Stanley to dinner. Junice had been angry because he had gone. They had been living together for two years and Junice thought it very rude of Jennifer to have invited Stanley over to dinner the night before their wedding and not ask her. When she complained about it one of her friends said, "You blind Junice ... blind, blind, blind."

"Blind? Blind about what?"

"Women don't ask men to dinner alone the night before they are getting married to another woman. Wake up, girl. Wake up."

Junice did not wake up until about six months after they were married, when Jennifer started calling the house and asking for Stanley. If he was not at home she would say to Junice, "You could ask him to call me, please?"

Days passed before Junice could bring herself to ask Stanley if he was having an affair with Jennifer. Stanley had denied everything, had cursed her for even thinking it, but Junice had opened her eyes and could see Stanley plainly for the first time. From that day on she did not trust him. She felt as if she had lost a big piece of herself that day, and she did not like it.

Junice had become pregnant soon after that. She had known at the time she had done it to feel that Stanley was really hers. She had felt terrified about being alone and did not want to go through learning a whole new person. Her first son did bring her and Stanley back to their original closeness. Though Junice still felt sad about his affair with Jennifer, she had told herself that he had ended it when he realised that she knew about it. She was wrong about that; Stanley had not ended the relationship at all.

One day when Junice was shopping in Yorkdale Plaza for a birthday gift and card for Stanley she ran into Jennifer in a card store. Jennifer stood reading a card and did not see her. Junice did not know what to do. She had neither seen nor spoken to Jennifer since she found out about the affair. She knew Stanley must have told Jennifer not to call him at home anymore.

Junice felt frozen for a second as she watched Jennifer busily making a selection from the section with cards for lovers and sweethearts. Suddenly Junice knew what to do. She moved back into the middle of the store and pretended to be reading cards while she continued to watch Jennifer. When Jennifer had finally made her selection and taken it to the cashier Junice moved quickly to her side.

"Hello, Jennifer. How are you?" she said brightly. "How's life? I haven't seen you or heard from you in ages! In fact, not since Stanley and I got married. You must give us a call and come over some time. I'm sure Stanley misses you. You haven't called lately."

As she chattered she quickly read the front of the card: "To My Darling Sweetheart On His Birthday." The card had a large bunch of red roses in one corner and was embossed in gold.

Jennifer stared at her, quickly collected her change and hurried out. Junice went back to the shelves and put back the card she had selected for Stanley: "With My Love On Your Birthday From Your Wife." It was a very simple card, black lettering on white paper, and there were no roses adorning it. She selected a card about the height of a two-year-old. It had gold embossed lettering and so many roses that it reminded her of an Italian garden. She winced and felt like shading her eyes from the shimmering gold lettering, but she paid for the card and gave it to Stanley the next day with vindictive pleasure.

She felt really pleased that she had dwarfed Jennifer's card. She did not tell Stanley about their meeting but waited to see if she could detect when Jennifer told him about it. She figured that Jennifer, who seemed to love to cook for men, had probably invited Stanley over for a birthday meal. Junice watched to see how he would try to juggle his schedule to fit what she had designed to be a packed day. His birthday fell on a Sunday. Junice invited her sister and her husband for Sunday brunch, and she lined up Stanley's closest friend and his wife for dinner. She also called up Stanley's mother and invited her over for the weekend, telling Stanley, "Your Mum sounds lonely so I told her she could come over for us to keep her company. She's longing to see you. She wants to talk to you about your Dad's grave in Barbados."

Manipulating Stanley's mother to fit into her plans had been easy. The first thing that Stanley's mother said when she saw him was, "Boy, I longing to see you. I was just saying dat to Junice in de car coming down." After she had sat down and was sipping a little ginger ale over ice she had said to Stanley, "Stan, seriously we have to talk 'bout you father grave."

Junice, busy in the kitchen, smiled with satisfaction. Stanley's mother always had something new to say about the tombstone, or the flowers on the grave, or the maintenance of the grave, or payment of the old woman who looked after weeding the grave.

Stanley managed to slip away long enough to eat at Jennifer's house. Junice watched him engineering it and said nothing, but another little piece of her died. As soon as brunch was over he had told her in the way that she now knew was his sneaky way of going off to do wrong, "I'm just going down the road. I'm coming back in awhile."

She reminded him that their guests were due in exactly two hours. He had said, "Oh, I'll be back long before that."

And so he was.

She wondered what he did with the gift he most likely received from Jennifer and where he put his gold-embossed card. She smiled to herself. In a way she felt as if she were watching a little boy playing truant. But he was not a little boy and she wept again as she drove aimlessly down the highway thinking about this incident.

Junice was expecting her second son when she saw Jennifer again. This time she was at a picnic at her sister's house. Stanley had opted to stay at home with their first child, who was recovering from his circumcision. They had postponed the operation because Junice said it was too much pain to put a new-born through. Now that he was three years old, the doctor persuaded her to have it done.

Stanley did not approve of circumcision. "It's not as good for men who are circumcised." Junice asked, "What's not as good?" "Sex," he answered, embarrassed. She was surprised that this man who was so wild sexually could be so prudish about talking about it. It used to irritate her that he was having an affair and hurting her to no end and could barely say the word "sex."

Before the operation Stanley again voiced his disapproval of circumcision. Junice stated flatly, "I'm not interested in making him enjoy sex. It's not the be-all and end-all, as you seem to think. I'm concerned about his health—that's what's important to me."

Stanley protested mildly, but the strength of his argument rested on what Junice called his "preoccupation with screwing," and he knew he could not win. He was very much involved with three women, yet Junice only knew of one. That made him feel guilty in a way that prevented him from arguing too loudly and too strongly with her.

He knew that Junice had waylaid Jennifer in the card store. After Jennifer told him he became worried and hurried back home the Sunday of his birthday. He knew, too, that Junice was watching him and had probably purposely arranged a tight schedule for the weekend. Stanley felt guilty about his affair with Jennifer after that. He wished there was some way he could explain to Junice why he truly needed Jennifer and truly needed Junice too. He loved them both in quite different ways and in quite different styles. The other women in his life were not important to him. He tried to compensate for the pain he knew he must be causing Junice and was much more loving and much more a stay-at-home than he had been. This made for problems with Jennifer, but he tried to make her understand the situation.

He wanted to put his foot down about his son's circumcision, but he did not want to risk what might come up if the conversation became any more detailed. Junice knew this. She knew, too, that she had won a round, but his giving up so easily further diminished him in her eyes. He had chosen to protect Jennifer at the expense of what he thought was best for his son. Another little piece of Junice died.

She was crying again as she drove; now they were quiet, trickling tears. She exited from the highway at Kennedy and made her way back to the west, towards home. She considered not going back, but she could think of no safe alternative, and besides, there were the children. She wondered where she would end up if she just kept on driving aimlessly on the highway.

She drove slowly along the road. A car horn tooted behind her, impatient with her slow pace. Junice increased her speed, but only slightly, and again the motorist blew his horn at her. Then he revved his engine and pulled up alongside her window by going out into the lane for oncoming traffic. Junice looked over in surprise as the car came up and the irate driver blew his car horn again to get her attention then gave her "the finger."

Junice felt so flat that she did not react. It was as if she had been given a welcoming jolt to her consciousness. She shook herself mentally and increased her speed. The irony of the situation struck her: she had received a hand back into her life from a most unlikely source.

As she turned her car into the entrance to her building she forced herself to breathe slowly. She thought of the children as she walked towards the building, swinging the car keys in her right hand, her left hand shoved deep inside her windbreaker. She had always liked the windbreaker; it was Stanley's and she had given it to him one Christmas before they were married. He had been so thrilled to receive it because he had always wanted one yet had never been able to afford one. They were students then and every penny had to be saved to pay for tuition and food and rent. After awhile he had stopped wearing it, but it was still his favourite jacket and he always told her that he liked to see her in it. That was one of Stanley's few demonstrations of sentiment. He was reserved, so cool. Sometimes Junice wondered if he was different with Jennifer. How could such a hot-blooded type put up with Stanley's reserve?

As Junice entered the elevator her heart felt a little lighter. She was anxious to see her children, and she could use the reassurance of Stanley's presence. At least the kids are here for me, she thought. But she was never the type to be thankful for small mercies. She needed the whole hog and she knew she did not have even the side-bacon.

In the elevator Junice said good morning to a tenant who was coming from the basement with a load of washing. She did not notice who the person was but had a vague sense of a white woman with her hair in rollers. As they rode together she realised the woman was staring at her, so she looked at her and immediately the woman began to speak, "You're Junice, aren't you?"

Junice nodded in surprise. People in the building spoke to each other, but they did not know each other's names, and certainly she did not think that anyone knew her name.

"I'm Celia. You don't know me," the woman continued, "but I know who you are because of your husband." Junice tried to look calm and still said nothing.

"Your husband is having an affair with my roommate and I'm very angry about it. It's unfair to you. I see you working so hard with your kids every day. I see you taking them to the daycare and I see you doing the laundry. I see you taking them for walks and I see you doing your grocery shopping alone. Sometimes while you're busy doing the laundry he's in our apartment, being entertained by my roommate. I don't want to upset you, but I'm so angry about these two people that I'm moving out this weekend. That's why I'm at home so late this morning. I took some time off to do all my laundry and packing."

The woman paused. Junice wanted to say something, anything. "So how long has this been going on?" she asked shakily.

"Ever since we moved in here, the week after you did."

Junice felt faint. Five years? Stanley had been with the woman for five years.

Punching her button on the elevator panel, Celia went on. "My dear, we moved into this building because your husband lives here. They were together before you got married. Then when you moved from the east end, because you didn't have a car yet, they decided that she should move nearer too. So we got an apartment in the same building."

Junice had retreated to a place outside her body. She saw herself leaning heavily on Celia's arm as she unlocked the door to her apartment and entered it. She wondered why she was going into Celia's apartment, then remembered that she had felt faint. She also wondered if the roommate was home, but she was too far removed from her body to ask the question; she could only shuffle into the apartment, still leaning on the arm of a woman whom she had just met in an elevator.

As they walked into the apartment another woman came out of the kitchen and stood staring at them. The second woman finally spoke. "What's going on?" she asked her roommate. Celia spoke openly about having introduced herself to Junice and about having told her about the affair with Stanley.

"I'm fed up with you and Stanley carrying on behind this poor woman's back." Distanced though Junice was, the woman's tone struck her as self-consciously righteous. She went into the kitchen and made Junice a cup of tea, then she said she would have to leave, as she had to get ready for work.

Junice felt a surge of energy. Once more at one with her body, she took control of the situation and sat up in her chair. "I want to know all about it," she said to Stanley's lover. She was surprised at the matter-of-fact way in which she spoke. She felt no anger, only relief and peace. The problem of what she should do about Stanley had begun her day. The solution had come unexpectedly and it had come from a most surprising turn of events.

Junice did not wince as the woman told her that she loved Stanley and had not been able to leave him even when he had told her that he was getting married. She did not think that Stanley loved her like she loved him, but she had still wanted to be with him, no matter how little of him she saw. She cried and Junice comforted her. She laughed hysterically once or twice and Junice touched her arm and calmed her. Then lowering her voice to a conspiratorial whisper, she told Junice she thought Stanley was falling in love with someone else. Lately he had begun to walk with a spring in his step and she believed he was seeing the new Trinidadian receptionist at work. She had accused him of it, but he had denied it.

Junice rather liked the woman. Her name was Renate and she was of German descent. She was big, strong, red-haired, with big teeth, which Junice at first had thought ugly, but as she watched her speak and laugh Junice thought that they kind of matched her long face, long arms and big feet. Yes indeed, I like this woman, Junice said to herself. She thought she understood what it might be like for some West African women who were co-wives. She decided to tell Renate about Stanley's affair with Jennifer.

While she was filling in Renate about Jennifer, Junice noticed the time on the kitchen clock. Putting her hand to her mouth suddenly she said, "My God, the kids! I have to take them to school!" She promised Renate she would call her and wrote Renate's telephone number on a piece of paper. "I suppose you have my number?" she laughed. Renate looked acutely embarrassed. Junice patted her arm and said, "Oh come on, never mind. I'm just pulling your leg."

Junice thought Stanley must be suffering from some form of lunacy to have brought a lover into their apartment building. She shook her head as she thought about it, wondering if Jennifer knew about Renate and determined to tell her as soon as possible. First she and Renate had some detective work to do, for they agreed to try to find out if there were any other women in Stanley's life and who they were.

At first Junice had been too shocked to talk openly with

Renate, but as she listened to her she felt a sisterhood with her. Stanley had met Renate when she was very vulnerable. She had just lost her husband in a motorcycle crash and she was lonely and sad. She had fallen in love with Stanley before he told her that he was getting married.

Renate's roommate, Celia, had come out of the bedroom just as Junice was saying goodbye to Renate at the door. Junice realised with a start that she was a very beautiful woman, much more beautiful than Renate. When Junice met her on the elevator she had been wearing a loose housedress and her hair had been in rollers. Now she could see the woman's long lashes fan out to touch her cheeks when she looked down. Her mouth was wide and sensuous and she had painted her lips a deep purple that contrasted with the turquoise of her dress. She had brushed her dark brown hair and let it fall onto her shoulders in a casual look that Junice figured had taken her a long time to achieve. With a satisfied smile on her face she said goodbye to Junice and Renate. Junice wondered about the smile because it did not look like the smile of someone who had just helped a friend.

Just after the roommate left for work, the buzzer from the lobby rang and Junice heard Stanley's voice boom over the intercom: "Listen, hon, Junice isn't home and I don't know where she is, so I have to take the kids to the daycare centre. They're in the car in the driveway already so I'll only be a few minutes. Meet me in the parking lot in about fifteen minutes."

"I'm not going to work today," Renate said into the intercom. There was a pause, then Stanley asked her if she was all right. Renate told him she was not feeling too well and that she would call him at work later. He rang off saying, "Take care of yourself, hon."

The two women looked at each other and laughed, although Renate looked a little embarrassed that Stanley had been caught out in front of his wife. Junice said, "My dear girl, it's all right. I have to take care of myself now, but I'm just so glad to have met you. I hope you can understand that I bear you no malice. I understand what happened to you—I'm a woman too. From what you told me, you haven't had an easy time and you haven't been happy either. I have no quarrel with you."

She looked over Renate's shoulder at a picture of Stanley on the wall next to the television set. He looks so weak around the mouth and the chin, she thought, I wonder why I never noticed that before?

Aloud she said, "You know, I still love him, but not stupidly and blindly. I believe that it's easier if you love a man with reality."

Renate said, "Then I better give you the whole picture. I wasn't sure if Celia could hear us speaking, but now that she's gone and you don't have to rush off to take the kids to the day-care, I can talk more freely."

The man Renate described did not sound like Stanley at all. He had been quite open with her about his other women, boasting that no woman could resist him. He had even told her about Jennifer, but she had not known her name. Stanley had five relationships going with women outside of his marriage and some of them had continued on and off for at least six years. Sometimes he would drop a woman and pick up a new one, but he always had a minimum of five relationships. Once Renate had quarrelled with a woman Stanley had had a relationship with for two years.

The woman worked in the same building as Stanley and

Renate, though not for the same company. One day when Stanley and Renate were walking into the building, the woman had started to curse Renate. She was Irish, and for awhile Renate had not realised what she was saying. After that incident Renate had tried to leave Stanley, but he would not let her go. He had come to her apartment so often that she had worried that Junice would find out. Then he had started to drive her to work every day. Before, he had been afraid that Junice would find out, but then he had assured her that Junice left home at least an hour before he did and Renate had eventually relaxed.

Stanley had been very attentive after that and she had had a hard time not forgiving him. One day when he smiled at her she gave in and smiled back. He knew that he had won her over again and that things were back to normal. Junice had known what she meant about that smile. What a fuss she had made about Jennifer when there were all those other women. Junice laughed, it felt good.

Renate offered Junice another cup of tea and she accepted. "Have you had breakfast?" she asked. When Junice shook her head Renate persuaded her to join her. Around mid-morning the telephone rang and Renate answered it nervously. It's Stanley, Junice thought; Renate is embarrassed for me. But Renate said, "Oh hi, Celia. How're you doing?" Junice could hear the relief in her voice and she noted, too, that Renate spoke loudly, as if she was intent on letting her know that it was not Stanley.

As the conversation progressed, Junice could see Renate's discomfort. I guess Celia's talking about me and Renate does not know how to tell her that I'm still here, she thought.

Junice decided to go to the washroom to give Renate the privacy to explain to her roommate that she was still at their apartment. When Junice returned she thought that Renate still looked embarrassed and maybe angry. Junice sat quietly, looking out the living room window, not knowing what to do. Then she picked up a magazine and started to leaf through it, quite unconvincingly, she knew, but she was becoming uncomfortable and did not know what else she could do to make it clear she was not eavesdropping. Renate was not saying much. Mostly "Mmm hmm" and "I see." Once she said, "No, not at all." Even if Junice had wanted to eavesdrop, she could not have picked up much.

Finally Renate rang off. "That damn woman." She threw her hands up in the air. "Why does she continue the pretence? Worse yet, why do I let her?" At Junice's puzzled frown, she said, "Let me tell you what's going on. At least it's what I think is going on. Celia is either after Stanley or she's already having an affair with him. I'm convinced of it, Junice."

Junice's shocked expression seemed to worry Renate. "Look, I don't mean to start anything. She brought you here to meet me and nothing is going to convince me it was because you were feeling faint."

"Well, she had already told me about you," Junice pointed out to Renate.

"Oh yes, of course. I forgot that. But when she said she brought you in because you weren't feeling well, I thought that it was an excuse to get you to see me."

"Maybe it was," Junice said, "but to be fair to her, I did feel faint when she told me about you and Stanley, and I did need a place to sit down while I digested the news."

She paused then looked at Renate with sharp eyes. "But do tell me, what's this about Stanley and Celia?"

Renate sighed. "I don't know where to begin. I've been convinced that he's hot and heavy in love with some new woman. At first I thought it might be that girl from Trinidad at work, but lately I've suspected it might be Celia. I can't swear that it's Celia, but several times I've come home to find her hanging up the phone guiltily. Let me see ..." she paused and looked down at the floor thoughtfully.

"For example, one day I came home early from a trip to Montreal and met Stanley just leaving my apartment, and he looked so guilty then that I wondered about it. Celia was in the shower and there was a strong smell of Stanley in the apartment. Junice, I don't mean to hurt you, but I've made love to Stanley—I know what a room smells like after Stanley has made love and that's what our apartment smelled like. I think they'd done it right here in the living room. But they both denied it and made me feel very bad for even suggesting it."

For a moment Junice felt herself leave her body again. "What could he be thinking of? How could he maintain a relationship with you and one with Celia, living in the same apartment?"

"Exactly," Renate said triumphantly. "That's why I think Celia is moving out and that's why she told you about me. It's a ruse to get both of us to leave him. She figures that she'll then have him all to herself."

Junice had not heard much more after that. She left Renate's apartment feeling lightheaded, feeling herself float to her own apartment. As she turned the key in the lock and opened the door, the dog jumped up to greet her. She welcomed its roughness. When Stanley phoned later that morning to ask her where she had gone so early and why she had not come back in time to take the children to daycare, she just said that she had been feeling depressed and had gone for a drive.

That evening Junice greeted Stanley quietly, unsure if he had been apprised of the morning's events. He seemed to be undisturbed and Junice wondered if Renate's suspicions were correct. If Celia's plan was for Junice and Renate to leave Stanley, then she would not tell him about her morning escapade. She would just sit back and wait. As the evening wore on, Junice became convinced that Stanley knew nothing. He took the children and the dog outside to the playground. After dinner he told her to relax and watch their favourite show on television while he washed the dishes. That made Junice suspicious, but when he joined her in the living room she looked at his face and saw no sign of anything unusual. She shook her head. No, she thought. He's just being nice—his once-a-month niceness, that's all. Besides, he's worried about where I was for the whole morning. She sighed and he looked at her curiously.

"What's wrong, love?" He always called her love when he was being his once-a-month nice self.

"Oh nothing," she said, letting it ride.

Much later when he turned to her in their bed she pretended to be asleep, even when he held her close and whispered in her ear, "I want you."

"I'm tired, Stanley. I've had a hard day," she said.

He said comfortingly, "That's all right." After awhile he said, "So where did you go this morning?"

Junice felt her body stiffen and so did Stanley. She could not answer right away.

"Were you all right? I realised that you had not slept well and I figured that you had gone out for a drive the way you sometimes do, but I got worried when you didn't come back in time to take the kids to daycare. Then I called you as soon as I got to work. What time did you come back? Did you go out for the whole morning until the time I got you?"

"Mmm hmm," Junice lied, feeling less like a liar because she did not say yes.

Stanley rubbed her back gently and snuggled up closer to her, but his touch was not sexual. "I worried about you all day," his voice was appropriately solicitous. "I even went to the day-care to pick up the kids in case you didn't make it there either."

He will not leave me, she thought, because I take care of his house and home and family. I'm The Wife. She sighed again. When she was younger she used to look at women who had become The Wife and wonder how they could stand to be so taken for granted. Before she met Stanley, she had been the mistress of a man whose wife had become The Wife. Then she had met Stanley and had broken off with the married man, who had claimed he did not get along with his wife. One day Junice spotted him and The Wife in the supermarket. The Wife was very, very pregnant and Junice's ex-lover was looking after her as if she were a precious jewel.

Now I'm The Wife, taking care of The Children and The Husband, she thought and sighed again.

"What's the matter?" Stanley asked, genuine concern for her in his voice. "Are you feeling bad about something, sweetie? Please tell me."

"It's nothing," Junice said. "Nothing at all."

She felt sorry for him she realised, sorry for Jennifer, sorry for Renate and sorry for herself. She even felt sorry for Celia because it was pitiful to have to be so devious and wicked just to try to get a man. She felt sorry, too, for all those other women who had been fooled by Stanley, for she had no doubt now that there had been others. She smiled at Stanley and patted his cheek. The next day while he was at work, she rented an apartment in Scarborough, moved her things, her sons and her dog into it and went to see a lawyer.

A Hard Choice

Vuy sat on her front steps eating a piece of black pudding. It was Saturday, and every Saturday she treated herself to Miss Hyacinth's black pudding. Today she muttered to herself as she ate: Every blessed day Stephenson come home from work, wash his skin, change his clothes and go back out until late night. Sometimes even one or two or three o'clock meet him out. On Saturday is even worse; he does get up in de morning, clean up de yard little bit and den begin to prepare heself to go out. First he clean his shoes, den he press his pants. And den he take out one of de clean shirts dat me iron dat morning and by two o'clock, he out in de street, strutting like some young cock.

Being so busy herself, it had taken her awhile to realise that she was hardly seeing her man. Now that she had noticed it she was very bothered but did not know quite how to handle it. She was determined, though, to put a stop to what he was doing.

Vuy was sure that Stephenson had a woman, and she planned to find out who she was. But what to do? She worried it around in her mind until she hit on a plan, which she decided to carry out that night.

Stephenson came home at seven o'clock that Saturday night, intending to change quickly and leave the house again. He had already prepared his clothes and had gone to make plans with his friends. As he entered the house, he met Vuy dressed to kill, sitting very still on a chair in the living room, back straight and her feet crossed at the ankles. For a moment Stephenson felt a chill as he looked at her. She had a cold, hard look about her that he had never seen before. He peered at her before he spoke. "Where you going?" he asked her.

"Out," she answered, exactly as Stephenson answered whenever she asked him where he was going.

Too surprised by her answer to say anything, he watched while she got up, picked up her purse and left the house. He went to the window and watched her walk down the street, thinking he should have done something to prevent Vuy from going out, but he was at a loss to know just what it was.

Vuy walked down the street laughing to herself. She was going to visit her sister, but she wanted to pretend to Stephenson that she was going to a party or some night spot so he would be jealous. She turned the corner and slowed her steps, not really feeling much like going anywhere, but she hoped that her plan would keep Stephenson from stepping out on her again, and she was determined to carry it out.

Her sister Alvira had agreed to help her out. If Stephenson asked her about Vuy's activities she would act stupid and pretend she did not know where Vuy had gone that night. They had laughed a lot about Vuy's plot and were looking forward to fooling Stephenson.

When Vuy reached Alvira's house she was surprised to find her sister's boyfriend, Presley, at home. He, too, had his nights tied up with a woman, but Alvira had accepted his carrying on years ago. Unlike Stephenson, who had to keep his other relationship hidden, Presley hid nothing. Vuy had told Alvira long ago that she should put a stop to it, but her sister had shrugged her shoulders, sighed and said, "Girl, Presley is a big man. If he feel to kill out heself wid woman, make him go ahead. He have asthma, too, so is only a matter of time. Besides, I going tell you de truth: it don't really matter if Presley come home late at night-time. If he don't even come, I don't really mind. You know why? I weary give him wife, Vuy, weary, weary, weary. I fifty-two years come July—you don't think is time for me to get some rest?" They had both laughed heartily at that.

When Vuy came into the house Presley looked at her in surprise. "Where you going, girl?" he asked. He had always made eyes at her; tonight he looked at her with open admiration.

Vuy gave him a cold stare. "I going out, but I just pass to see Alvira." She did not want Presley to know her business, since he could let it slip to Stephenson later. She just hoped that he was not staying home. Soon Presley got up, went into the bedroom and began to change his clothes. Then he left, saying to Alvira, "I coming back just now."

As soon as he closed the door behind him Alvira gave a little wry laugh, "You hear de gentleman? 'I coming back just now.' Sometimes you wonder who dese men tink dey fooling. He conscience prick him tonight, is so you still meet him home."

She paused and there was some of the old fire in her eyes as she spoke again, "Before you come he tell me he tink he might stay in tonight, but as soon as he see you he so glad for a excuse he dress and leave."

She shook her head and there was no mistaking now the anger in her voice. "He fool heself and tink me have company so he can leave even though you tell him say you not staying."

Partly out of compassion for her sister, Vuy moved the focus to her own problem. "Well, I leave Stephenson home wid his eye popping out his head. His mouth open two time to tell me someting, but his mind don't know what to say." She laughed and looked out of the corners of her eyes at Alvira to see if she had made her smile. Alvira's face still looked grim.

Vuy continued, still hoping to get her sister to enjoy the joke on Stephenson. "He just watch me as me walk up de street. I sure he watch me till I turn de corner and long gone. But girl, I didn't look back tall, tall. Only Lot wife one did look back and you know what happen to she: a straight case of pillar of salt."

At last Alvira's sense of humour surfaced and the two sisters giggled at Vuy's joke. Taking some glasses from the china cabinet, Alvira brought out Presley's rum. She called her son in from the street, where he was playing with his friends, and sent him to the shop to buy two bottled sweet drinks. When he returned she fixed herself and her sister a drink, saying, "I want you go home with rum on you breath. Dese men must frighten because dey don't have no conscience. If you don't frighten dem early dey take advantage of you."

Before Vuy left Alvira washed out their glasses so Presley would not know they had been drinking his rum. Then laughing tipsily she threw some cold bush tea into the rum bottle to bring it back up to its former level. Vuy, too, laughed at the doctoring of the rum bottle, then she left for home, feeling quite tipsy. As she neared home Vuy saw the lamplight burn-

ing. Stephenson was home. Though it was late enough for her
to have felt uncomfortable walking down the street by herself,
it was early for Stephenson to be home. He never came home
after a Saturday night out until after two o'clock on the
Sunday morning.

She did not believe that her going out had upset him
enough to make him give up his night out. She thought that
maybe his friends must not have picked him up. As she
opened the door to the one-room house she saw Stephenson
lying fully dressed on the bed. He turned quickly to look at
her. Obviously he had fallen asleep without meaning to,
because he still had his shoes on.

"Girl, you now coming home! What happen to you, you
crazy?" Vuy did not answer and Stephenson advanced on her
threateningly, "Vuy, is you I talking to. Where you went to? I
even go Myrtle party go look for you."

Vuy had not known that Myrtle, his cousin, was having a
party. She supposed that Myrtle had told Stephenson about it
and that as usual he had gone to it by himself. She did not
answer but turned and gave him a strong look. Heaving her
chest at Myrtle's treachery, she thought: Myrtle is one of dose
women who invite de man to de party and don't tell de woman
anyting tall 'bout it. She know full well dat when she do dat,
de man can choose to leave you home if he feel like it.

As she began to take off her clothes Vuy shook her head
in resignation, still not answering Stephenson, who stood
waiting. Too shocked to speak, Stephenson looked at Vuy
with real puzzlement. He kept on grumbling and complaining,
but still Vuy said nothing. She just looked at him every now
and then, sometimes defiantly, sometimes coolly.

When she had put on her nightie and got into bed Stephenson took off his clothes and got into bed beside her. He put his arm around her and kissed her. Vuy lay still. He smelled rum and sniffed at her mouth.

"Vuy, you smell stink a rum!" he exclaimed, moving away from her, although he could not move very far and stay on the little bed. Vuy got up and brushed her teeth and still said nothing to Stephenson. She climbed back in bed silently and put herself at the edge of the little bed. She was frightened, but she could not give in now for she would lose all the work she had put into the night. The rum helped; it dulled the edge of her fear. Soon she was snoring loudly.

Stephenson sighed in exasperation and left her alone. He did not know how to handle this Vuy who had gone out alone on a Saturday night and had returned home so late smelling of rum.

The next morning Vuy got up and made breakfast for herself and Stephenson as if nothing extraordinary had taken place. Stephenson was still hoping to be offered an explanation. By the time he had finished eating his breakfast at the little bedside table he could wait no longer. "So where you went last night, girl?"

Vuy said quietly, "When you go out I don't ask you nothing. Well, when I go out don't ask me nothing either. If is so you want to live we can live so."

She felt quite proud of her answer and not at all afraid. She decided to speak her mind entirely. "Understand I not living in no house wid no man who coming and going as he like and me trap inside house. No, no, no. Nothing tall go so. Dat not fair cause I not living like so wid you, and besides, is me own house. You not coming inside de house me old mother leave give me and giving me horrors."

Stephenson's silence was helping her to feel even stronger. Last night she had been frightened, but having won that first round, she was strong and resolute. "You feel you could make me into some kind a fool, nuh? Me must take you in, take you right in me heart, cook for you, wash for you and you just coming and going as you please? You enjoy dat life Stephenson? What life is dat for me?"

She looked at him but did not wait for an answer. Taking a deep, deep breath, she continued, "Better I live by myself and you live on you own because me not enjoying no companionship wid you and you just using me."

It was the longest speech Stephenson had ever heard Vuy make and the most she had ever said to him on the subject of his staying out. It was not like her at all to bawl him out or to hold up her property as a threat. On the contrary; she had always referred to her house as "our house," and he had come to feel he was part-owner of the little house that Vuy's mother had left her. After all, when he had wanted to borrow some money from the bank to buy his truck, Vuy had taken the house deed and had gone with him to the bank.

Stephenson looked at her face carefully. Last night he had wondered if she had another man, but he did not think that now. "Vuy, you vex because I does go out sometimes?"

Vuy laughed, a little crazily Stephenson thought. "Sometimes? You call dat sometimes? Stephenson, you does go out every blessed night dat God make. You don't stay home wid me tall, tall. Me never see you tall until late night or early morning when Friday and Saturday come. You treat me like one hotel, you not treating me like you woman."

She paused then turned to look at him full in the face. "Me sure you have some next woman somewhere," she said. "You have a next woman, Stephenson?"

By now she had stopped eating breakfast and was sitting on the steps leading out to the yard. Tears were running down her face. Stephenson got up from the table and sat down next to her. "Is so, Vuy," he said. "Is so. I don't mind to stay home more, but me not giving her up."

Vuy heard herself telling Stephenson to leave her house. The next day, after Stephenson had taken his things out of Vuy's house in his truck, he came back to see her to promise her that he would pay the loan that she had signed with him. She nodded, not trusting herself to speak, and as soon as he had gone she went to see her sister. Alvira argued, "Vuy, you sure dat you had to take it so far? I don't mind you did go so far as to give him a nudge or two, but how you make de man move out? He is not such a bad man."

Vuy looked at Alvira sitting alone in her living room at nine o'clock at night, knowing that she sat there night after night. "Yes, Alvira, I did have to take it so far. I not living wid no man who just using me. I not going give him shelter, wash his clothes, cook his food and den he not even dere wid me when night come. Before so is best I get a child because at least me pickney not going running off night after night after night."

Alvira looked at her sister thoughtfully and nodded. "Is hard. I does go through it meself and I understand, girl. De ting is, too, after awhile you just accept de situation and den is too late."

Alvira got up and took two of her best glasses from her china cabinet. She rinsed them out and dried them. She took some ice from the little fridge in the front room and put two cubes in each glass. Then she called her son and sent him to the shop to buy two bottled sweet drinks.

Soon the two sisters were sipping rum and sweet drinks. Vuy tinkled the ice in her glass. "I miss him already," she said. "Is a hard choice," Alvira said. She sipped her drink again, sure she was tasting something odd in it. Noo noo balsam? No, she remembered, she had topped up Presley's rum with bush tea. She reminded Vuy about it and they were laughing when there was a knock at the door.

Before she even caught sight of Stephenson's face, Alvira had recognised his knock and was saying, "Come in, Stephenson, come in."

Unsure about what to do, Vuy started to cry. "Let's get married, Vuy," Stephenson said, kissing away her tears. "Let's get married, den we will work things out. I don't want to lose you, I rather lose de other woman."

Vuy's eyes met her sister's over Stephenson's shoulder. Then she said, "Is a hard choice, Stephenson. Is a hard choice."

Made in the USA
Charleston, SC
08 December 2009